...OMA VALLEY

TAHOMA VALLEY

by

C.E. Osborn

This is a work of fiction. Names, characters, businesses, places, events and incidents are either the products of the author's imagination or used in a fictitious manner. Any resemblance to actual persons, living or dead, or actual events is purely coincidental.

Cover design:
SelfPubBookCovers.com/Viergacht

© 2022
C.E. Osborn
All rights reserved

For Brian H.

CHAPTER 1

"Zach, are you still packing up your truck?"

Zach looked up from the list in front of him and nodded in the direction of Autumn's voice. "Yes," he called out.

The reality show *Creature Hunt* was nearing the start of filming another season. As the host, Zach had been busy since his return from a trip to Oregon in June, looking over notes for some of the locations he'd be visiting over the course of the next three months. He and his girlfriend, Autumn Hunter, had realized they wanted to go somewhere together before he left, and had decided to take a few days to join her friends in a familiar place.

The small town of Tahoma Valley, where Autumn and Zach had met a couple of years ago, was a well-known area for Bigfoot sightings. Autumn had been asking Zach since June if he'd join her when she decided to go with her group, and it was now late August, just a week before Labor Day. He had agreed, and was looking forward to it, but there was one thing he and Autumn had not yet fully agreed on regarding the trip.

"Almost done," he replied as Autumn appeared beside him. Her reddish blonde hair was almost gleaming in the sunlight. She smiled and squeezed his arm. "Listen, Autumn, there's something we need to talk about again."

"Erica, Mike, Bill, and Nate are all staying in the cabin across from us," she said, knowing what Zach was about to say.

"I know. You told me that this morning." He counted out six trail cameras and placed them into the built-in gear box in the truck bed. "I just want to make it clear that we're not going back to the cave. The only time I plan to be around it is when I set up and take down the cameras. We know what's there. We know the creatures are territorial and dangerous. I'm just looking to possibly get some footage on audio or video, and interview some of the locals in the area."

"Do you think my backpack is still out there?" she asked,

looking at his checklist. "It's been two years, so it's probably disappeared by now."

"I would think it's gone. Along with everything that was inside."

She nodded. "Zach, I'll try as hard as I can to not go back down there. Bill and Nate brought it up, and they were very enthusiastic about attempting to visit the cave again and get some pictures of the creatures in their home. Erica is being cautious about it, just like you are."

"They may have moved on," he pointed out. "Just because people think they're still seeing Bigfoot doesn't mean that they are."

Autumn laughed. "It's still so hard to believe you can be such a skeptic with all the cryptids you've actually seen."

Zach knew there was a contradiction between his experiences and his beliefs. His time spent interviewing witnesses for the show had convinced him that people could see an otherwise familiar animal in unfamiliar surroundings and let their imagination do the rest. Still, he had often encountered many other people whose experiences he had never questioned.

"I understand their point of view, but I'm doing all I can to be a passive observer this time. I'm bringing trail cameras, audio recorders, digital cameras, flashlights if we want to go exploring closer to the cabins again, bear spray, a couple of knives, and some other equipment we might find useful."

"I think that sounds like everything we'll need. We'll be staying at Mitzi's resort again, so we don't need tents or anything like that."

He closed and locked the back of his truck. They had chosen a quiet neighborhood when they had been looking for a home together, but some of the neighbors occasionally walked past the house and stopped to stare. They knew who he was, and what he did for a living, and a couple of times people from a few blocks away had seen him outside and started chatting with him about an episode they had watched.

"It's almost time to call Sherry," he said. "I know she'll

say no, but I want to make one more attempt to get the production company to come out to Tahoma Valley."

He closed the truck bed door and swung down the glass canopy window. He had asked for some specific equipment while buying the truck, and it was well-fitted if he ever needed to take it into the backcountry and camp out. The two of them had already taken it down to a campground near Mount Saint Helens to look for a return visit from a rumored Batsquatch, but the creature had failed to appear this time. Zach swore he had seen it on his trip in June, and Autumn believed him.

Autumn followed Zach into the house, picked up her cat, Squatch, and settled down in the recliner in his den. She wanted to hear for herself what the show's executive producer would say when Zach proposed an episode of the show be filmed in Tahoma Valley. Zach sat down in front of the computer and set up a video call to Sherry Anstrom.

"Hi, Zach," she said, looking surprised when she answered and saw it was him. "I wasn't expecting to hear from you."

"I'm going to be away for a few days, and thought I'd check in before I go," he explained. He told her about the rise in Bigfoot sightings in Tahoma Valley, and that he was going out to explore the area. "Last time I was out there I had a couple of encounters with a Bigfoot," he concluded. He had mentioned the story to Sherry, but hadn't been quite as forthcoming as he was being now. "Is there any way the crew could film an episode there?"

She looked down at some papers on her desk, then back up at him. "We can't do it, Zach."

"Why not?"

"We already have a tight filming schedule, which starts in two weeks. Everything's lined up. We can't just pull the crew in and film an entire episode in a small town on almost no notice."

Zach nodded, feeling disappointed. He had known it would be a long shot to get the show to travel out here. Just off to the side, out of the view of the web camera, Autumn shook her head. She leaned back into the recliner, careful to not make any noise.

"Sherry, I'm telling you, this could be big."

"So could any of the other locations we're going to this season."

Zach looked away from the computer, and raised his eyebrows at Autumn. There was an alternative they had discussed, although he wanted to make sure she was agreeable to it. She nodded. "Go for it," she whispered.

"How about this, Sherry? I don't have to report for filming for two weeks. What if I go ahead and do this myself, with a group of local investigators? Would you be willing to turn that into an extra episode of *Creature Hunt*?"

Sherry looked intrigued by the idea. "I won't make any guarantees, Zach. If you come to us with interesting footage and ideas for what to do with it, we'll talk about it."

Zach nodded. "Thanks, Sherry. I'll see you in a couple of weeks."

"Bye, Zach."

The screen went blank. He turned to Autumn. "I meant what I said about this investigation, Autumn. We're going to be as hands-off as possible."

She nodded. "In truth, I'm not all that crazy about being up close with Bigfoot again. It would be nice to find out what happened to all those blood and hair samples I collected last time."

Zach checked the time. "Hey, let's go out for dinner. Italian?" He named one of her favorite restaurants. They changed their clothes and left the house for a relaxing evening, knowing the next few days would be a rush of investigating and looking for proof of a monster's existence.

"Come on, Mike. Pick out a candy bar and let's get back to the cabin."

Mike Morris glared at his cousin, Bill Morris. "Just give me a minute, okay?" He placed two bars on the counter and then looked at the rest of the selection again.

Bill sighed. "Erica's going to wonder if we were kidnapped by Bigfoot or something."

Mike saw two men on the other side of the store, standing near a map of the area, glance over at them. "Keep it down."

Mike and Bill were in Tahoma Valley with their friends Nate Parker and Erica Morelli to follow up on some Bigfoot sightings they had been reading about online all summer. They had arrived a day earlier than their friend Autumn and her boyfriend, Zach, because they had been able to get a good deal on an extra night in the cabin.

"Do you think we should go down to that cave again?" Mike asked as he finally picked out the last two candy bars and paid for them.

"We'll have to discuss that with the others," Bill said, looking around. He smiled at Mitzi Taylor, the owner of the resort, as she gave Mike his change. "We love the cabin, by the way."

"Good. I hope it's comfortable," Mitzi replied.

"It is." Bill guided Mike out the door with a hand on his shoulder. In the corner, near the map, the two other men looked at each other with wide eyes.

"The cave. Isn't that what Tony was talking about, Aaron?" one of them asked.

"Yep. Looks like that bunch already knows what's down there," Aaron replied. "Let's head back to the cabin, Cal. Tony said he had something to show us." They smiled at Mitzi as they left, and she shook her head. They had been in and out of here all day, and hadn't yet bought anything.

"Are all the Bigfoot hunters gone?"

Mitzi turned and saw her husband Marvin entering the general store. The store sold soft drinks, beer, candy, snacks, and a few fresh sandwiches to the people staying at Mitzi's Cabin Resort. It was shortly before closing time, and starting to get dark outside. Most of the families that had been staying at the resort during the week had left, and several more groups were coming in tomorrow. It had been a profitable summer, with the common theme of "looking for a monster" at the heart of several return visits.

"Not quite," she said. "That Tony Simons guy and his two friends checked in last night. Autumn Hunter and Zach Larson will be here tomorrow, staying until Wednesday, and their friends already checked in today. They're out in Cabins One and Two, away from all the others."

Marvin nodded. "Seems like the Bigfoot craziness has died down for the moment."

The store door opened again. This time, Deputy Reilly Brown stepped inside. He was one of several sheriff's deputies that patrolled Tahoma Valley and the surrounding towns. He had grown up here, and knew most of the townspeople by name. That helped him when there was trouble, because people trusted him. His frequent partner, Joey Singleton, a female deputy patrolling the region for a few years, had become almost as well-regarded in the area.

"Hey, Marvin. Mitzi," Reilly greeted them. He stepped over to the drink coolers and found a couple of bottles of soda. Mitzi joined him at the register.

"Busy night?" she asked.

"Not really. No calls of drunken escapades over at the tavern, or shoplifting at the grocery store. Joey's off for the evening, so it's just me out there for now."

"Someone else on duty at eleven?" Marvin asked.

"Yep." He paid for his soda. "Hey, do you have a guest here named Tony Simons?"

"Yes," Mitzi said. She would not have answered the question for anyone except law enforcement. "Why, are you expecting trouble from him?"

"No. He came into the station a couple of months ago, and also visited Carson over at the clinic." Dr. Carson Smith, his father Stan, and his brother, George, were all long-time residents of Tahoma Valley. "I thought I recognized his car when I passed by one of the trailheads earlier today."

"He's here with two friends," Mitzi confirmed.

"We might have some excitement in the next few days,"

Marvin commented. "Zach Larson is coming back to town."

Reilly paused before drinking his soda. "Is that so? I would have thought he'd be busy with that show of his."

"You remember Autumn Hunter?" Mitzi asked.

Reilly smiled. "I'm not likely to forget her. She came back nearly a year after her first visit to try to find the backpack she lost, claiming we had locked it away in a vault and that it contained evidence she needed to prove Bigfoot exists."

Mitzi nodded. "Yep, she and her friends stayed here for a few days right around then. Her friends checked in today, and Autumn and Zach will be here tomorrow."

"I wonder if we're going to see Tahoma Valley on the show," Marvin mused.

"Autumn didn't say anything about it when I talked to her," Mitzi said. She looked at the clock. Marvin nodded and turned the sign on the door over to "Closed."

A car drove into the resort, slowing down once it pulled off the highway. "One of the guests," Mitzi said, recognizing the dark gray sedan. "A young woman, Talia something. She's in the cabin next to Tony and his friends."

Reilly gave her an amused look. "If Zach were to put you on *Creature Hunt*, Mitzi, he'd have to devote half an episode to your appraisals of all the Bigfoot hunters you've seen come through here."

Mitzi laughed. "I'm not sure they could safely air my opinions of most of them." She followed the sedan with her eyes until it disappeared behind the tree line. "Tony, though, seems very research-oriented. I wonder how he and Autumn and Zach get along, if they know each other."

"I'm sure they know each other," Reilly said. "I'm also sure they're all going to be looking for the same things in the same places, and that can cause some tension."

His radio came to life, and he gave a brief response. "Time to hit the road again. There's a disturbance out at the campground. Fourth time in the last month. See you both later." He waved as he left. Marvin locked the door behind

Reilly, and he and Mitzi cleaned up the store and counted out the register.

The two of them left the store together and walked down the dirt path to their house. It was set back behind the office, and not easily seen from the road. Mitzi liked the privacy. She enjoyed talking to the tourists that came in, but when she was off-duty she wanted the same type of retreat that her cabins offered.

"Do you think Zach and Autumn are going to get what they're looking for this time?" Marvin asked when they were relaxing on their couch. "Proof of Bigfoot?"

"I don't know," Mitzi admitted. "I'm not sure I want to be the place that's first been proved to be the home of a Sasquatch. Can you imagine how much Tahoma Valley would change?"

Marvin nodded. They had each had their own supposed sightings of the creature, and had kept that to themselves. "Maybe we should tell Zach what we've seen," he suggested hesitantly. "It can't hurt, and I doubt it's anything he hasn't already heard."

"Okay," Mitzi agreed, so quickly that Marvin knew she must have had the same thought. "Now, I think it's time for bed. We have a busy week ahead of us."

"What's going on over there?" George Smith asked his girlfriend, Jessie Harris, as they saw a crowd of people near a campsite. They had come to the lake today to swim and take a break from their normal routine. Jessie had a rare day off from her job as a waitress at the Valley Tavern, and they had been at Rainier Lake Campground, soaking in the sun and playing in the water, for almost seven hours now. George was tired, full from the picnic dinner Jessie had packed, and was ready to get back to his house.

"I don't know," Jessie answered, squeezing his hand. They had to walk past the people on their way back to the parking lot, so they slowed down to see what had caught everyone else's attention.

An RV was parked in a site, and two people who appeared to own it were chatting excitedly with Deputy Reilly Brown. He had pulled his car up in front of the camper to block anyone else from approaching the campsite. Once George was able to look around at the site, he stopped and stood still.

The bed of the pickup truck, now unattached from the RV, had been hit multiple times by something strong. Three large dents ran along the side of the vehicle, and a cooler stood on its end, obviously now empty. One of the screens on the camper had been torn away from the window, in a location that George assumed was close to the kitchen. The couple had set up three chairs around the fire pit, and two of them had been tossed clear over to the edge of the forest, nearly thirty feet from the camper. There were also a couple of dents in the camper door, and a torn screen on that window.

"What could have done that?" a voice asked from the crowd. George and Jessie looked at each other, knowing full well what kind of creature could have attacked the camper. It was the fourth such attack in the campground this summer. Some monster out there was looking for food, and it was very hungry.

"Damn, Devontae, are you sure we should sleep in our tent tonight?" a woman asked her boyfriend, a muscular man standing next to her. "Maybe we should pack up and go. If something attacked the camper, our tent doesn't stand a chance."

"It's late, Tracy. I'm not leaving," the man said. George silently disagreed with the man, but didn't say anything. Bigfoot had probably already gotten what he wanted for the night.

"If you're sure," the woman said, doubt evident in her voice and face. They walked away from the group, and other people dispersed soon after, realizing that the deputy was just getting information from the campers.

Finally, Reilly shook their hands and turned away from the couple. They went back into the trailer, studying the dents on the door before closing it. George waved at Reilly as the deputy came around the side of his car.

"Hi, George," Reilly said. "Good to see you. Hi, Jessie. Having a nice day off?"

"Yes!" Jessie said brightly. She knew what was going to be bothering George later in the night, and wanted to try to get thoughts of the local monsters out of his head. "Finally got too dark, so we're headed home."

"It was here again, wasn't it?" George asked quietly. "Bigfoot."

"The couple only saw what they described as a tall, furry, man that appeared to only have one hand," Reilly said cautiously, looking at his notes. "The creature looked at them and ran off with some fish in its possession."

George had had a similar thing happen to him more times than he wanted to think about. He looked at Jessie's face and smiled, trying to clear his thoughts. "Well, I'm glad you're looking into it and not me."

"Me, too," Jessie said. "Let's go, George."

She took his hand and led him back to the car, chatting about her co-workers and what they had probably put up with from the local men at the tavern that evening. George half-listened to her, recalling the scene at the campsite. When they got into his truck and started to drive back to his house, his thoughts came back into focus.

His father still lived down near the cave that the Bigfoot seemed to call home. The repeated incidents at the campground made George wonder what was going on down there, and why the creature was venturing out in more public spaces in recent months, causing sightings to rise and bringing Bigfoot hunters into town. He'd go down and see his father tomorrow and try to sort out the reason behind all the new incidents. With that settled, he put his arm around Jessie and she leaned against him for the rest of the ride home.

CHAPTER 2

"Damn, it's getting dark out here," Talia Harrison muttered to herself. She turned on her headlights and pulled out onto the highway, leaving the cheerful lights and mood of the Valley Tavern behind her. It was a few miles back to her cabin, and she hoped to get there before the day really caught up to her.

Last night she had been a very happy woman. That was before her boyfriend called to tell her he was staying late at work. A woman had spoken in the background, and her words had chilled Talia. "Oh, why keep lying to her, baby?"

Talia had paced around her apartment, then decided it was time for a change. She had been working non-stop for several months and needed a break. She had called her boss to tell him she was using a couple weeks of vacation time, packed her bag, and cried herself to sleep.

This morning, she had set out early for the serenity of the small towns and open spaces near Mount Rainier. She had only been in this area a few times, but after locating Tahoma Valley on a map, it had sounded like a good place to relax. She had come across Mitzi's Cabin Resort on the way into town, hoping that there would be a vacancy. There had been one, and she had unloaded her bags into the small wood-sided A-frame cabin next to the creek.

After taking a few moments to sit on the back porch and stare out into the forest, Talia had a small breakdown. She had cried and paced for a couple of hours, then took a nap and woke up hungry. She had only brought a few candy bars with her, so after stopping at the general store to ask Mitzi how to get to town, she had shopped at the grocery store and treated herself to dinner at the tavern. There had been a few groups of what seemed to be locals, but otherwise she was surprised at the sparse crowd for a Saturday night. She had assumed the tavern would be filled with loggers and hunters telling each other stories about what they had encountered that day.

She was now in a better mood, and laughed away her assumptions of the town. Her cabin had a hot tub just off of the back porch, and as she continued on her drive, she started thinking about getting home and relaxing in the tub while stargazing. It would be a clear night, and she hoped she might see a deer or two wandering past her cabin.

An animal abruptly entered the road. Talia saw it just in time to slam on her brakes. The unexpected jolt against the seat belt caught her in the chest. "Ow!" she shouted. She looked out the windshield to see what she had almost hit.

It was a huge wolf. As she continued to stare, though, she noticed it didn't look like any wolf she had ever seen before. Its back paws were longer than most canine paws, and the front paws extended into long, finger-like claws. The animal had brown hair, and she could see a small portion of its back that was healing from a wound. An almost round patch of hair and some skin was missing, leaving what would probably become a large scar on an otherwise smooth hide.

The wolf stared at her, then continued on past her car and into the woods on the other side of the road. As it reached the edge of the forest, it shocked her by standing on its two hind legs and turning around to look at her car. Its long snout moved back and forth, and its yellow eyes blinked a couple of times. Then, it bared its teeth. "What the hell?" she asked herself. Sheer instinct made her press the gas pedal. She did not want to see this creature any longer.

She drove slowly and looked in her rearview mirror. The wolf was now back in the middle of the road, somehow still standing on two legs. She knew that was she was seeing was impossible, and it scared her. Headlights appeared in the distance, and the creature disappeared. It seemed to have had enough human contact for the evening.

"What? What?" she asked herself as she continued down the road. She found Mitzi's resort and slowed down. There were a couple of vehicles, along with a sheriff's truck, parked at the general store, but she passed on without stopping. She didn't think anyone in law enforcement would believe her if she told them she had just seen a wolf walking on its hind legs.

She drove slowly, looking for the path that led to her cabin. When she found it, she carefully looked around at the forest as her headlights illuminated the rock-filled road. She realized she was expecting the wolf to suddenly jump out, as if it could recognize her car and had followed her over here.

She pulled up in front of her cabin and was glad she had left a light on outside the door, as well as inside the cabin. She took a moment to assess the situation. Her keys were right in her hand, and she could run straight from the car to the door and be within the solid walls of the cabin in just a few seconds.

A movement made her glance to her left, and she breathed a sigh of relief. The cabin closest to her was occupied. She had seen one man sitting outside earlier in the afternoon, and now there were three of them on the porch, looking over at her with some concern. She took a deep breath and got out of the car.

"Hello!" she called out, glancing behind her at the forest. "Nice night, isn't it?"

"Yes, it is," one of the men answered with a smile. He stood and walked to the edge of the porch.

She heard a sudden rustling in the bushes beyond her cabin and decided to get away from her car. "May I ask you a question?"

"Sure, come on over," the same man said. He was a little under six feet, with black hair cut short, and wearing jeans and a long-sleeved shirt. His companions were also wearing jeans and t-shirts. One was blond with a buzz cut, and the other had reddish hair down to his shoulders.

"Thank you," she said. She hoped she wouldn't sound crazy to them, but figured she would rather approach a stranger with her wild story, and risk being laughed at, then being told that she was wasting the sheriff's time.

"My name is Tony Simons. These are my friends, Aaron Robb and Cal Parker." Tony folded a piece of paper he had been looking at and set it down on the ground. He smiled at her again. She felt a sudden attraction to him.

The redhead waved. "I'm Aaron."

The blond raised a bottle of beer in her direction. "I'm Cal."

"I'm Talia Harrison," she said.

"Is this your first time in Tahoma Valley?" Tony asked. He gestured for her to sit down on the extra chair that was on the porch.

"Yes. I found this place by chance," she said. "Have you been here before?"

"A few times," Tony said. "We're cryptid researchers."

"Cryptid researchers?" Talia echoed.

"Would you like a beer?" Aaron asked. "We also have hard cider."

"Cider," she answered, with relief. Aaron removed a fresh bottle from the nearby cooler and opened it, handing it to her. She drank the cold liquid and felt both relieved and intrigued. "Okay, what are cryptids?"

"Have you ever heard of Bigfoot?" Cal asked, his voice serious.

"I think pretty much everyone living in this state has heard of Bigfoot at some point," Talia said. She had never paid much attention to the stories, but it was hard to avoid mention of the large furry ape that supposedly roamed the woods of Washington.

"Well, that's just one example. The Loch Ness monster is another. There are stories all over the country, and the world, of creatures that science hasn't identified or classified."

"So that's what you're trying to do?" Talia asked. "Look for those monsters and prove that they exist?"

"Yes," Tony said. "I work at a biology lab that sometimes gets samples sent in from various wildlife agencies, and we're asked to run tests to identify the species."

"It's common that the samples turn out to be bear, or wolves, or just regular dead domestic animals," Aaron said. "Sometimes it's not as easy."

Talia shuddered at the mention of wolves, and took a sip of cider. Luck had led her to these men, who would probably not laugh at her. They may not think what she saw was a cryptid, but at least they wouldn't think she was crazy. "What about walking wolves?"

"You mean werewolves?" Cal snorted. "Not likely."

"Or do you mean a different kind of creature?" Tony asked, with a glare at Cal. "Have you seen an animal that was doing something you weren't expecting to see?"

Talia nodded. His soothing demeanor, and the way he leaned forward, urged her to keep talking. One more sip of the cider gave her the courage to tell them what she had encountered on the highway. "On the drive back here, I was on the highway and an overly large wolf crossed the road. I stopped, and when it was done crossing, it paused, turned around, and stood up on its hind legs."

Tony's eyes gleamed. "Really? Tell me everything you remember about it."

She closed her eyes and related the large paws and elongated fingers, the wound on the back, and its snout and yellow eyes. "It seemed to be sniffing the air to see if it could smell me," she said, opening her eyes again. The men seemed transfixed by her story. "I made it back here and saw you, and was relieved to have other people around. I decided to take a chance that you might know something about it. Or, that you wouldn't laugh and call me crazy."

"I've heard about similar creatures," Aaron said. "I think they're sometimes called upright canines, or dogmen."

"Or wolfmen, by people who insist on believing in that nonsense," Cal said. Talia got the sense that he was the most skeptical of the group.

"We know people have seen Bigfoot around here," Tony said. "Yours is the first report I've heard of that involved a dogman."

She shivered, both from the night air and from recalling the creature. "I hope I don't run into it again." She stood. "Thanks for the cider. Okay if I take the bottle with me?"

"Sure," Tony said. "Hey, if you'd like to learn more, would you join us for dinner tomorrow night at the Valley Tavern?"

She studied the three men. She was here to get over her ex-boyfriend's betrayal, and Tony was attractive and seemed intelligent. She had already trusted the men with her story. She was sober enough to decide that she would drive herself to dinner and meet them at the tavern the next night. That way, she could leave if she found herself in an uncomfortable situation.

"Sure," she said. "I'd like to look around the area in the afternoon, by myself. How about we meet there around six?"

"Six," Aaron echoed.

"See you then," Tony said. He winked at her, and she blushed.

Talia took the cider and walked over to her cabin. She was no longer fearful, and lingered outside long enough to make sure the car was locked. She waved to Tony, then opened her front door. She felt better knowing that the three men were outside, watching the clearing. Once she was inside, she drew all the curtains and decided against using the hot tub. Instead, she curled up on the couch with a book.

Once Talia was in her cabin, Cal whistled. "Well, she just added some excitement to our trip"

"What do you mean?" Tony asked. He retrieved the floor plan of the local medical clinic, which he had had folded and put away when Talia had approached them.

"Well, she's attractive," Aaron said. "She seems to be interested in you, Keep flirting with her and maybe she'd be willing to help us. There's also her story."

"A dogman?" Cal asked with a heavy tone of skepticism. "You really think that's what she saw?"

"She didn't have any reason to lie to us," Aaron argued.

"Not until she heard we were Bigfoot hunters," Cal replied. "You know how people suddenly come out with the wildest tales they can imagine when they hear that."

"Speaking of Bigfoot hunters, another group from the

Bigfoot Online Group is here," Aaron said. "Autumn Hunter's friends. They were talking about the cave you want to find."

Tony looked up. "You think they're going to go looking around down there?"

"Probably," Cal said. He finished his bottle and opened another one.

"Then Talia might come in handy," Tony said. "I bet Autumn's going to be here as well. I can talk Talia into distracting her, and that boyfriend of hers if he shows up, while we go down and get a look at Bigfoot."

Aaron and Cal looked at each other. "How are you going to do that?" Cal asked.

Tony shrugged. "Money. That always works."

Cal set down his beer. "Let's figure it out in the morning. What's going on with your plan for that hidden room you've been talking about?"

"I think the entrance is here," Tony said. He placed the detailed plan on the table in front of him. Aaron and Cal both got up and looked at the drawing. Tony had drawn the map from memory after a trip to Tahoma Valley at the beginning of the summer. He had made up a reason to see Dr. Carson Smith, and had received a tour of the clinic.

"The entrance to the so-called secret vault?" Aaron asked. "Where?"

"In Doctor Smith's office. This door is probably a supply closet. I think this other door, the one I saw next to the bookcase and that was painted to blend in with the wall, leads to the vault."

"How did you hear about this in the first place?" Cal asked.

"You know how people talk when they think no one is listening," Tony said. "One of the sheriff's deputies, Reilly Brown, was denying the existence of such a place to a tourist when I stopped by the station to ask for directions. After the tourist left, Deputy Brown turned to another officer, Deputy Singleton, and muttered that word was getting out."

"So, you think you'll find some sort of solid proof of Bigfoot in there," Cal said. "Maybe a skin or hair specimen?"

"The lab has received samples from this area in the past," Aaron said. He worked in the same place as Tony, although Tony was the more experienced researcher. "It makes sense that they keep the samples somewhere when we send them back."

"So, when do you want to pull off this crazy stunt?" Cal asked. "And who's going down into the vault?"

"Today's Saturday. How about Monday night? I'll find a way to fake an injury, and Aaron can stay in the exam room with me. We'll do it later at night, when there's fewer people on duty. While we're busy, you can get past the front desk and look in the doctor's office for the key, head down into the vault, and find something to bring back to the lab."

"We're really taking a dangerous chance that there's something there to begin with," Cal said. "But it sounds like it might be fun to try."

"That's why we brought you along, because danger is your idea of fun," Tony laughed. "Okay, I think that's it for tonight. Time for bed."

The men headed inside. Tony went up to his bedroom, while Aaron and Cal stayed downstairs to watch television. They flipped past several channels, including a marathon of the show *Creature Hunt*. They were sure they would get enough of hunting monsters before the week was over.

CHAPTER 3

When Zach reached Tahoma Valley, he stopped and pulled off the highway onto an unpaved strip of land. A large sign welcomed everyone passing through, or vacationing in, the small town, and gave an estimated population of a little over five thousand people. Zach figured that was about right, although given the proximity to Mount Rainier, he was sure that the number would almost double during the summer months.

He retrieved the video camera from the passenger seat and filmed the sign, then got some footage of the highway. He tried to think of what his normal cameraman, Brandon, would be looking for, and panned around. He turned it off when another vehicle approached, slowed, and then sped up again, revealing a family inside. A boy, probably around ten years old, stuck his tongue out at Zach as the minivan passed.

Zach smiled and drove further into town. The first place he stopped was a large strip mall, where most of the commerce in Tahoma Valley was located. He remembered the grocery store, the ice cream shop, the diner, and all the other smaller stores standing around the central parking lot. Someone visiting could get anything they needed here. He saw a gift shop with a flag hanging in the window, featuring a cartoonish waving Sasquatch. For a wild moment, he contemplated buying one for Autumn, but knew she would never let him hang it up at home.

He followed several people into the grocery store and browsed the aisles with a cart, looking at the list Autumn had made and adding a few items as he passed them. The cabins had basic appliances and some dishes in the small kitchens, so they could easily make some meals on their own. He found a bag of his favorite chocolate candy and put it in the cart, then added another type of candy for Autumn. He finished up in the beer and wine section. They'd only be here for a few days, so he bought six-packs of some hard cider and beer, and a single cold soda for him to drink in the truck.

After paying at the register, he placed everything inside one of the coolers in the back of his truck and once again got out the video camera. Many people had their phones out and were taking pictures, so he didn't feel out of place as he panned around the center, then got closer to the gift shop and got some clearer shots of the flag, and the window display that included several Bigfoot items. He saw t-shirts, a hooded sweatshirt, books about the creature, and lots of small figurines and keychains with the creature on it.

He left the strip mall and returned to the highway. A mile or so down the road, he saw a park with several people sitting at picnic tables and lounging on blankets, with kids playing on swings and playground sets. A group of men, most wearing jeans and t-shirts or tank tops, sat on lawn chairs near the park entrance. Right under the sign for the park, someone had put up a banner, white with black letters, proclaiming "NO BIGFOOT HERE" in all capital letters.

Curious about the sign, he stopped and parked just inside the fence at the entrance. He grabbed his phone and walked over to the sign, getting some pictures of it. "You one of those Bigfoot people?" a man called, standing up at his chair. He wore a gray t-shirt.

Zach wondered how he should answer that. "I guess," he admitted. "I'm interested in Bigfoot."

"Lots of people have been through the forest here this summer, causing trouble," the man said. His friends seemed content to let him speak for the group, but they watched the conversation with interest.

"I can promise you I don't want to cause trouble," Zach said. "I'm curious. Is this sign a warning to tourists or to Bigfoot?"

One of the other men laughed. The guy in the gray shirt glared at him and turned back to Zach. "Tourists, of course."

"So Bigfoot is welcome in this park?" Zach asked. He couldn't help himself. This was the first time he had encountered a situation like this.

"I saw a dead one not too long ago," another one of the

men volunteered. He stood and walked closer to Zach. He was wearing a dark green shirt, and Zach saw a logo on it that identified the county sheriff's department.

"You did?" he asked. This was big news, if it was true.

"Briefly," the man admitted. "I was out hunting." He lowered his voice. "Not someplace I was supposed to be. My cousin is a deputy and I don't want to get him in trouble."

"Understood," Zach said. He gestured for the man to follow him, and they walked over to Zach's truck.

"I know who you are, but I didn't know you were coming back to town," the man said. "I'm Chase Brown."

"Zach Larson. I assume Reilly Brown is your cousin?"

"Yep. Anyway, I was down by the cave near old Stan Smith's house. It was getting close to sunset, and I was on my way out of the woods. No luck that day. Then, I tripped on what I thought was a log."

"What was it?" Zach asked eagerly, keeping his voice down.

"Just what I told you. It was the body of a dead Bigfoot." Chase's voice wavered, and he closed his eyes. "I saw an ape-like face, and its arms were long, hanging down close to its knees. It was on its side, and at first, I thought it was just sleeping. Then I noticed the long claw marks on its leg, and the chewed-out throat." He opened his eyes again. "Some other animal got to it, but I don't know what could take down something that size."

"Brown!" the guy in the gray shirt called out. Chase held up a hand to let his friend know he had heard him.

"Anyway, I got out of there. I didn't want to be anywhere close to that body if something came looking for it. I wouldn't be surprised if someone else came across the remains, too. I haven't been back there since."

"When was this?" Zach asked.

"Maybe a couple of months ago," Chase said. "I gotta go back with my friends. Good luck with whatever you're doing here." He shook Zach's hand and hurriedly walked back to his chair, pausing only to say a few words to his friend.

Zach got into the truck and drank his soda, thinking as he swallowed the cool, refreshing liquid. This was something he had never heard before. He was sure that the body would be long gone by now, but if it had been down by Stan's house, then the older man might know something about it. He would go over there this afternoon and see if Stan could give him any more information. He also wanted Stan to know that he'd like to put up trail cameras in the area.

He drove through the rest of town and, a few miles down the highway, he pulled his truck into the main parking lot at Mitzi's Cabin Resort. It was half past noon, and he saw a few families stocking coolers with ice and drinks, probably just bought at the on-site store, before heading out for picnic lunches.

He walked up to the door and looked through the glass. A teenage girl was at the counter, her side turned to him, restocking the candy section. A sign posted on the door with tape directed guests to check in at the office. As he turned around, he smiled and nodded at a couple of people who seemed to recognize him. Two middle-aged men waved hesitantly, and he waved back before turning to his right to go to the office.

The front room of the one-story white cement building was wood-paneled and cooled with a ceiling fan. Marvin sat at the desk and smiled when Zach closed the door behind him. "Hello, sir!" he exclaimed as he stood and shook Zach's hand. "It's nice to see you again."

"It's good to be back here," Zach replied. He sat down and took in the pictures on the wall. Most of them were of Mount Rainier taken from different angles. One photo showed Mitzi and Marvin standing next to a large statue of Bigfoot, one that Zach thought he recognized. "Is that in Seaport?" he asked. "I was just down there in June."

Marvin nodded. "Yep. Mitzi and I went down a few months ago, before the weather started getting really nice up here."

"Who looked after the resort?"

"George Smith volunteered for the task," a warm voice replied from behind him. Zach turned and saw Mitzi standing in a doorway leading to what looked like a lounge. "And he did a great job. Between him and Carla, the girl from town who comes in to help us out, this place didn't miss a beat."

Zach stood again and hugged Mitzi. "Autumn reserved a cabin for us."

"Yep." Mitzi walked around to Marvin's side of the desk and pulled a folder from a pile on the edge. "Cabin One, where you stayed last time."

"Good," he said. "That had a nice view across the creek and it was quiet."

"Autumn's other friends checked in yesterday," Marvin said. "I was worried they may feel crowded in Cabin Two, but they insisted it was fine."

Zach smiled. He knew Mike, Nate, and Bill were used to staying in a camper, so being in a two-bedroom cabin would seem almost luxurious for them. Erica would have insisted on the cabin no matter where the others slept. "I'm sure they were happy about the space." He pulled out his credit card and gave it to Marvin. "Have you seen or heard anything creeping around the woods here?"

"We noticed that there's a pile of tree limbs across the creek that seems to have been built over the past few weeks," Mitzi said, a hand on her hip. "Not as big as some structures over there in the past. The only noises we've heard were some howls, but there are wolves that come through this area sometimes."

Zach retrieved his card and looked over the rental agreement. They had decided to stay until Wednesday, which should be enough time to gather some photos, video, and get in a couple of interviews. The price was reasonable, and he noticed that Mitzi had given him and Autumn a discount. He wasn't going to argue, because he was fairly sure it was an argument he would lose.

"Anything else you've heard about?" he asked. "I'm sure you've had some Bigfoot hunters here recently. Autumn told me there was a rise in sightings earlier in the summer."

Mitzi and Marvin looked at each other. Mitzi nodded, and Marvin sighed. "A couple of weeks ago, some guests told us that they saw a few splashes of blood on a tree, along with what seemed to be a pawprint."

"Pawprint?" Zach's interest was piqued. "Where was this?"

"Close to where that structure is, on the other side of the creek" Mitzi said. "The blood was washed away. I went out to check on it myself, just after I heard about it."

"Did you find anything else?"

"A piece of what appeared to be animal flesh. It was small, round, and ragged, and whatever animal it's from probably was hurting for awhile."

"Most likely two animals fighting over food or territory," Marvin said. Zach was struck by how that sentence could apply to anything from raccoons to large mammals.

"Well, I better get to the cabin," he said. "Autumn should be in this afternoon. She ended up having to go into work for a couple of hours, so we decided I should check in and start getting our equipment set up." He shook hands with the Taylors, then left the office and returned to his truck. He drove past the store and down the path that led to the secluded clearing housing Cabins One and Two.

Mike and Nate were sitting on their porch when Zach pulled up in front of Cabin One. He waved to them, then unlocked the door and removed his luggage from the truck. Autumn's bags were next, and then he hauled the cooler inside and returned to the truck. He stood at the tailgate, looking in the back and trying to figure out what else to bring into the cabin.

"Need any help?" Erica asked from his side. He turned and greeted her with a hug. She was a couple of inches shorter than Autumn, with curly brown hair. She and Autumn had been friends for many years, and both of them shared a deep interest in Bigfoot. Erica was much more hands-off than the others in her group, preferring the role of observer, which made her a good person to be monitoring any cameras in the area and to let someone know if anything appeared that should be investigated.

"I think I have everything I need for now," he said. Mike, Nate, and Bill approached. Zach looked into the box where he had placed some of the weapons. He pulled out the bear spray, a knife, and a couple of flashlights. Bill saw the bear spray and nodded.

"Mike and I just bought some tasers," he said. "We're kind of hoping we get to try them out this week."

"On animals, right?" Zach asked. He was only half-joking. Sometimes on trips like this local people came into the forest while he was exploring, and the noise they made had his senses on alert. One of his crew members had accidentally tased someone last season, an action which everyone involved regretted.

"Of course. Although, if Tony Simons gets close enough, I might find a reason to use it on him."

Zach looked around. "Nate, where's Tiffany?" She was Nate's long-time girlfriend.

"She wasn't able to get the time off this week, but made me promise I'd check in every day," Nate said. "I guess just so she can be sure I'm still alive."

Zach laughed. "I'd probably be asking Autumn to do the same thing if I wasn't here." He loved Autumn, but sometimes her determination to go into dangerous situations was a source of frustration between them. "Tony Simons. That sounds familiar."

Erica filled him in on Tony's history with their group as she followed him into the cabin. The others drifted back to Cabin Two. "And he's here with two of his friends, the same people he was with last time. Autumn's not going to be happy about it, but all we can do is try to keep them apart."

"Agreed," Zach said "How about we have dinner tonight at the Valley Tavern, around six? We can figure out a plan for the next few days."

"The guys already have some ideas about that," Erica

said. "I'll show their list to Autumn. See you later." She waved and left. Zach waited until he saw her enter the other cabin, then grabbed his cell phone and walked outside. He headed behind his cabin and down the gentle slope to the creek, then sat on a boulder to observe what was going on across the water.

From here, he had a view of the trail that led down to one of the town parks. He knew Autumn and the others had explored it in previous years. In the clearing at this end of the trail, there had once been a log structure, similar to the one described by Mitzi, that he had taken pictures of. All of those pictures had been removed from his camera by Deputy Reilly Brown and Dr. Carson Smith. Both of those men were trying to protect the town by hiding or eliminating evidence of Bigfoot. Autumn thought they were keeping things in a hidden room somewhere, and Zach had now come to that same belief.

Three men came into view on one side of the clearing. One had dark hair and tan skin, another had reddish hair that was long and pulled back from his face, and the other was blond and looked like he had come out of the military with his buzz cut. They were all examining the pile of branches that Mitzi had told him about. The larger structure was long gone, but the limbs that were carefully put together now evoked the same sense of shelter as the other habitat.

"Tony, there's a print over here," the redhead said excitedly. Zach watched as Tony Simons eagerly strolled past the structure and along the creek bed, further away from Zach. The men took photos, then suddenly turned around as if finally sensing the presence of another living being.

Tony gestured to Zach and quietly said something to his friends. The three men slowly walked in his direction, although they stayed on the other side of the creek. "Hi," Tony called. "Are you Zach Larson?"

"Yes," Zach admitted. "Have we met before? You look familiar."

"I'm not sure. I'm Tony Simons. This is Aaron and Cal."

The others waved. "We're here in town to follow up on some evidence of Bigfoot."

"What evidence would that be?" Zach asked.

"Footprints, and some hair samples."

"Hair samples?"

Tony nodded. "I'm deeply interested in trying to prove the existence of cryptids. If we could start with Bigfoot, a creature that has permeated cultures around the world, maybe people wouldn't be so skeptical about other monsters."

Zach almost found himself agreeing with him, but remembered what Erica had told him about Autumn's encounters with Tony. "My girlfriend is trying to do the same thing. Have you heard of her? Her name is Autumn Hunter."

Cal and Aaron both gasped, but looked down at the ground when Tony stared at them. He turned back to Zach with a smile pasted onto his face. "She and I are both members of the Bigfoot Online Group, but we have different opinions on the best way to do field research."

Zach nodded as if he really believed Tony. "Okay."

"We better get back to the cabin, Tony," Cal said. "It's lunch time."

"Always have to follow your stomach," Aaron grumbled.

Tony nodded. "I agree." He and the other guys crossed over the creek near Zach. "Don't worry, we won't be passing through this spot often. The creek widens and narrows again near our cabin, so we usually cross there."

"Good deal," Zach said. "See you guys later." He watched them disappear around the bend, then hurried across the narrow body of water to look at the limb structure himself.

It appeared that the limbs had been torn from trees, rather than cut down or gathered from the ground as would be expected if a human had put them together. They all pointed up and were weaved together to form a shelter that would mostly keep out the rain, and would provide protection from the sun. He heard voices, and walked back over to the trail. Several people in the distance were taking pictures of the forest and chatting with each other.

A Bigfoot would be risking detection and scrutiny from humans by building a structure here. He had felt the same way the last time he had seen one in this clearing. He didn't know why the creatures would need a shelter up here, when he was nearly certain that at least one of them was still living in the cave at the end of Forest Hill Road, by Stan Smith's house.

Thinking of Stan made Zach smile. The last time they were here, the Bigfoot had seemed to be lurking around the older man's house quite often. It in Stan's front yard that Autumn and Zach had experienced their first sighting of Bigfoot, and Stan had drawn blood from the creature while trying to get it to leave the property.

He went back to the cabin and ate a sandwich, then cleaned up and put some equipment in his backpack. The cameras were still in the truck, so he left a note for Autumn and set out for Stan's house, hoping Autumn would be arriving soon. He was anxious to get the rest of their investigation under way.

CHAPTER 4

Zach approached Forest Hill Road and slowed down. He had noticed a tall fence that started along the highway about a quarter of a mile back, and now he understood why the fence was there. "Private property," he read out loud. "No trespassing. Dead end road."

The turn-off onto the road was an open space. The fence started up again on the other side and came to an abrupt end roughly fifty feet down. He turned onto the gravel-filled road and stopped again, getting out of the truck to look around.

He walked along the fence until he came up against a chain-link border. Someone had gone to great lengths to keep the general public away from here. Stan Smith's house was the only residence down here, a simple but well-furnished log cabin, so Zach started to feel excited as he imagined the possibilities.

He returned to the truck and continued on down the road. He saw the log cabin, and he waved to the older man sitting near the empty fire pit, under the shade of a nearby tree. There was an empty chair beside him, and another truck parked in the driveway. Zach recognized the vehicle and was glad that George Smith was there, as well. He had a question for him.

"Well, I think I remember you," Stan said as he stood up from his canvas chair. "Hi, Zach. What brings you back to Tahoma Valley?"

"I'm here to look into some rumored Bigfoot sightings," Zach said, shaking Stan's hand. "And to see what's going on down by the cave again."

"The cave?" a familiar voice said. Zach turned and saw George standing behind him, carrying two glasses of iced tea. "Hi, Zach. What's this about the cave?"

"Autumn and her friends are going to be here for a few days with me," Zach said. "Remember Autumn?"

George set the glasses down on the table and took a seat next to his father. He sipped his tea and nodded. "Very smart young woman. She was intense about Bigfoot."

"Both of those are still true," Zach laughed. "She and I have been dating for over a year. Anyway, she monitors online discussions about Bigfoot, and pays close attention to sightings near Mount Rainier. She noticed a lot of people were talking about Bigfoot up here this summer. I have some time before I start filming the new season of the show, so we thought we'd come here and set up some cameras to see what we could find."

"There hasn't been that much activity," George insisted.

"George, you know that's not entirely true," Stan replied. "You were here with me just last week when we heard sounds coming from the woods behind the house. Strange calls, like wolves, but louder and meaner." He looked Zach in the eye. "Are you worried those creatures will remember you?"

Zach hadn't thought about that possibility. "No," he said, but he heard the doubt in his voice.

"There were three creatures there the last time you were in the cave?" Stan asked.

"Yes," Zach said. It had seemed like a family unit, with two older creatures and a younger one. The young one had stolen Autumn's backpack, which had held nearly all the evidence collected during that weekend.

"We're pretty sure there's only one now," George said. Zach looked at him in surprise. "The one whose hand you cut off."

"How is it surviving on its own?" Zach wondered out loud. "And why do you think it's the only Bigfoot left here?"

George looked down at his glass. "I've taken a couple of hikes down there this summer. I think…" his voice trembled, as it had before when he had spoken about the creatures. "I thought I saw a dead Sasquatch body. And another time, I thought I saw the wounded one standing near the cave, behind a tree."

"Why didn't you tell me anything about this?" Stan asked.

"Sorry, Dad. I just wanted to get out of there."

"When did you see the body?" Zach asked.

"In June, around the time a lot of sightings picked up around here. It was already decomposing, but I could tell something had ripped out its throat. By the time I got up the courage to look for the body again, it had disappeared." He shrugged. "That happens. Nature takes care of it. Scavengers eat the body and the bones get scattered and buried."

That matched Chase Brown's story. Zach was glad it was George who had seen the body, because he trusted the other man to be completely honest with him. He hoped George would be willing to share more about it on camera.

Stan looked at George for several moments, then cleared his throat. "You got a whole camera crew here with you?' he asked Zach.

"No. The producers from my show didn't want to come here and film an entire episode, so part of what I'm doing is essentially making one on my own. Is it okay if I come back in the next couple of days to interview you?"

"About what happened a couple of years ago, or what's going on now?" Stan asked.

"Possibly both."

"It's fine with me."

Zach turned to George. "It might be easier for you to come and see us at Mitzi's. You told me your story the last time I was here. Are you willing to share it with the world?"

George looked down at the ground, taking a long time to respond. When he looked back up at Zach, there was determination in his eyes. "I'll talk about some of it, but I don't want to bring any harm to Harry's family."

"I understand," Zach said quietly. George had lost a close friend in a Bigfoot encounter twelve years ago, and he could see that it was still a difficult topic.

Stan cleared his throat. "I assume you noticed the signs and the fence?"

"Yes, I was going to ask you about that. Who owns this land now?"

"I do," Stan said proudly. George cleared his throat, and

Stan winked at him. "Well, I own part of it. George and Carson put in the money for the rest. That way it can continue to stay in the family for as long as we can hold on to it."

"When did that happen?"

"Last summer," George said. "It took a while to put up the fence, but there was no objection from anyone in town. They know what happened at the cave a couple of years ago, and they had already been warning people away from them."

"Every now and then a car comes down this way," Stan said. "The trailhead and parking lot are still down at the end, and I don't say too much unless I start thinking people have been down there too long. We've only really had trouble once, with some drunk college kids that were daring each other to take a night hike."

Zach nodded. "It sure made me slow down. I only continued on because I knew you lived here." He looked at a couple of the trees near the road. "Hey, do you two know anyone who might have a possible monster sighting to share?"

"You might want to talk to Jessie, over at the Valley Tavern," George suggested. "She and I have been seeing each other. She said that she may have seen something other than a Bigfoot in the last few weeks."

"Other than a Bigfoot?" Zach repeated. "Did she describe it?"

"Only that she thought she saw something standing behind a row of tall ferns, behind the tavern, that was thinner than she thought a Sasquatch should be. It must have seen her, too, because she said it suddenly dropped down, and she heard rustling like it was crawling away along the ground."

"Was this at night?"

"Nope, after a day shift. Late afternoon."

Zach nodded. "I'm having dinner there later. I'll try to get a few minutes to speak with her."

"There was someone driving past the cabin earlier, going in the direction of the cave," Stan said. "I didn't recognize the car, but it went back the other direction shortly after I saw it. Maybe they saw the deserted lot and chained-off path and realized that there was nothing worth looking at."

"A Bigfoot hunter changing his mind?" George laughed softly. "Not likely. Probably just lost."

"If you don't mind, I'd like to put one of my trail cameras on the tree at the end of your driveway," Zach said. "I'm heading down to the cave to set up a few cameras down there as well."

"No, I don't mind. Who's going to be looking at the footage?"

"Me, or one of Autumn's friends. The camera up here, and a couple of others down the road, will just take pictures if someone or something moves past it. One of the cameras down by the cave will also work on a motion sensor, but will film five minutes of video if it's triggered."

"You're not going alone," George insisted. "I'll come with you."

"I'm not so old that I don't like a bit of adventure," Stan said. "Let's all three head down the path, and hope those creatures aren't out looking for a mid-day fight."

Zach retrieved one of the trail cameras from his truck and attached it to a tree right at the end of Stan's driveway. He took the others and joined George and Stan in George's truck. As they drove down the roughly paved road toward the parking lot at the end, Zach felt he was being watched. He was glad he had made the decision to let technology do the observation work this time, but he knew that at some point he and Autumn would be out in the woods around town.

The three men got out of the truck. George took his shotgun from behind the back seat, made sure it was loaded, and carried it carefully as he followed Zach and Stan to the trail that led down to the cave. Zach looked around and found a perfect tree for the camera. He stretched up and snapped the strap tight, tugging to make sure it could withstand some force if something tried to pull on it.

"Are you sure it's up high enough on that tree?" Stan

asked doubtfully.

Zach stood back and shrugged. "It's the best I can do."

They started down the trail, constantly looking around at the brush along the sides of the path. By the time they reached the cave, Zach was feeling nervous, and wanted to get out of the area as soon as he could. He stood on a rock and placed the video camera against the tree, once again making sure the strap was tight. He noted the locations in the notepad app on his phone, then pulled up the footage and nodded. "A deer just ran past your truck, George," he noted, looking at the digital photo that had just come in.

"Great. Let's go."

Zach looked at the trail that led up the hill. "Where did you find the Bigfoot body?"

George stared at him. "Why?"

Zach shrugged. "I'd like to know."

"I'd like to know, too," Stan said.

George turned and led them to the lower trail that ran past the cave. They walked single-file down the path, each taking care to step as quietly as they could. They were out of sight of the cave when George stopped and pointed down at the ground in front of them.

"Right here," he said. "Like I said, it had been dead for a while when I stumbled over it."

"Have you heard about anyone else seeing it?"

George shook his head. "No."

Zach wandered off the trail for a few feet in each direction, looking at the ground around him. He heard Stan and George chatting quietly behind him. He saw nothing, and was disappointed. Part of him had hoped that a trace of the Bigfoot might have been left behind.

"I think we should go," George said suddenly.

Zach nodded. The three men retreated back down the path, taking care to be silent as they walked past the cave entrance. In the daylight, even under the shade of the tall evergreen trees, it was not an intimidating place. If Zach didn't know a monster might still be lurking in there, he would have felt comfortable suggesting that they explore for a few minutes. However, both George and Stan ignored the cave and he followed them, not wanting to be left behind. Shortly before they reached the truck, they heard rustling not too far off the path.

"Think it's another deer?" George asked softly, bringing his gun up to his chest.

"Maybe," Stan replied. A low growl penetrated through the bushes, and Zach froze. He had heard that sound before, and it was something he had not expected to hear this week. He knew the usual howls and roars of a Bigfoot. This was not the same creature.

"Let's get to the truck," he said out loud in a forced casual manner. Stan and George nodded and they hurried back. Once they were inside the vehicle, Zach sighed with relief.

"All sorts of things growl out here," Stan said. "Could that have been a wolf?"

Zach debated voicing his concern. He finally decided that the fewer people who knew there could be another dangerous monster in the area, the better chances he might have to get some footage. And, there would be fewer chances for an encounter.

"Possibly," he said. "I've heard they come through here from time to time."

"Listen, just let me know if you or any of the other people in your group want to come down here," Stan said. "I may not think it's the best thing to possible stir these creatures up, but at least if I know someone's here, I can come down and do what I can to protect them."

"I'll let the others know," Zach said. "I told Autumn I wanted to limit our potential contact this time, and she agreed. I have a feeling her friends might not be so content with that."

They went back to the cabin and George got out another chair for Zach. He spent a couple of hours chatting with them, hearing about the town and about the summer people who always tried to suggest changes for Tahoma Valley. He set up an appointment with George to come over to the resort the next day to be interviewed on camera, then checked his watch. It was time to head back and pick up Autumn for dinner.

"Thanks for everything," he told them. "I'll be in touch."

"Good luck, Zach," Stan said. Zach nodded and drove back up the road. He had two trail cameras left, and coming to the fence gave him an idea. He stopped and tied one to a fence post, facing down the road. They could see if anything crossed the road onto Stan's land…or left it.

CHAPTER 5

Autumn was relieved when she finally pulled her sedan into Mitzi's Cabin Resort and got out at the general store. She had been called into work shortly before she and Zach were scheduled to leave, with her boss claiming only she could solve a problem that had come up. She had taken only a few minutes to do so, but she had already told Zach to go on ahead of her, so he had left the house. All her bags, except for her purse, had been with him, so she could simply leave straight from work.

The drive through town had been filled with families pulling on and off the road, and she had slowed down to stare at a sign declaring "NO BIGFOOT HERE" and wondering if she should stop to talk to the group of men sitting beside it. Her desire to get to the cabin had been too strong, so she had continued on and decided to ask Zach if he had also seen it.

Two families exited the store, with the kids holding ice cream sandwiches and the adults chatting about packing for the drive home. She walked around them and entered the store. It was now empty, except for the middle-aged smiling woman at the register.

"Well, hello, Autumn! Zach checked in a few hours ago," Mitzi said. "And you managed to catch me in a rare moment of peace."

"It's been busy here?"

"Summer is usually pretty busy, but the cabin requests the last month really picked up. I had to turn away a few people, and even relocated two couples to house you and your friends. I knew you'd probably be out late doing some outdoor research and thought you'd want the privacy of Cabins One and Two."

"Thank you very much," Autumn said, feeling grateful. "Those two cabins are so set apart from the others that hopefully any activity won't disturb anyone else."

Mitzi leaned under the counter and produced a key. "You and Zach are in Cabin One. Your friends are in Cabin Two.

I normally only have two or three people sleeping in that one, but Erica assured me it wouldn't be a problem."

Autumn nodded. Erica would take one bedroom. Mike and Bill, the two cousins, would take the other bedroom, and Nate had insisted he'd be fine sleeping on the couch. They had already texted her a picture of their computer and audio set-up, along with all the groceries they had brought along for the three days they were planning to occupy the cabin.

She picked a couple of diet sodas from the cooler, and paid at the counter. "Have you been seeing anything strange around here, Mitzi? Heard any noises you couldn't explain?"

The older woman laughed. "Zach asked the same thing. I did remember something after he left the office, though."

"What's that?"

"We heard something prowling around the dumpsters a couple of weeks ago. My husband opened the back door of the store and saw what looked like the biggest dog he's ever seen loping off towards the forest, with an awkward gait. He called out to me, and I made it to the door just in time to see the dog or wolf disappear, and seconds later we saw a tall shape rise against a tree trunk, standing on two legs and watching us. We shut the door and waited several minutes before leaving and going back to the house."

Autumn was stunned. She was familiar with witness descriptions of dogmen, and she shivered briefly as she remembered her own up-close encounters with more than one of the canid cryptids. "I'll be sure to tell Zach. Thanks, Mitzi."

"Have a good stay, Autumn. Let us know if you need anything."

Autumn nodded and left the store. She drove down the resort road and turned off into the area that held Cabins One and Two. They were set apart from the rest of the resort buildings by a thick patch of forest. It was an ideal setting for their group, as she knew the others would insist on being out in the woods at least one night to see if they could get anything on audio or video.

She parked and entered her cabin, smiling at the typical mountain lodge decorations. Zach had left a note on the dining table to let her know that he was going to talk to a couple of people, and set up trail cameras, and would be back around five. She checked her watch. That gave her an hour and a half to unpack and talk to her friends.

She found her bag on the bed upstairs and unpacked it, getting her clothes and toiletries settled into the bedroom and bathroom. She checked her backpack for all of her gear, and once again wondered if the pack she had lost two years ago was still down at the cave. Satisfied, she took her key, locked the door behind her, and headed over to the other cabin.

Erica answered her knock. "You made it!" She reached out and hugged her. Autumn smiled in her friend's embrace. They hadn't been able to spend much time together in the past few months and had jumped at the chance when Nate had suggested they come up here see if they could add to the stories on the BOG forum. The Bigfoot Online Group, or BOG, was the online cryptid discussion forum where Autumn and her friends spent most of their time discussing and reading about Bigfoot and other creatures.

"Mike, Bill, and Nate went for a drive down the highway. They'll be back soon. Zach dropped by after he got settled in and we all agreed to meet at the Valley Tavern for dinner a little after six."

"Sounds good. What other plans did you all come up with?"

Erica led Autumn to the dining room table and Autumn looked at the neatly written list they had put together. "They're going down to the cave?"

"They'd like to, just to look around on the paths above and next to the cave," Erica said. "I know you told Zach you wouldn't go down there, but they didn't make that promise to him. So, Mike figured they'll go while it's daylight, take some pictures, and then leave."

"What about you?"

"No thanks. Not after your experiences there."

"Nate wrote down 'Back to the clearing' here."

"At some point, either tomorrow night or the next night, the guys agreed to go back to that patch of woods behind the cabin and set up some audio. Tree knocking, vocalizations, that kind of thing. We did it the last time we were here."

"And we attracted some of the local wild guys," Autumn recalled. "Hopefully they don't show up again."

"Oh, and here's something you probably didn't want to hear," Erica said. "Tony Simons and his friends Cal and Aaron are also staying here at the resort."

"Upgraded from the campground, huh?" Autumn said. "Well, we should have guessed we'd encounter them again at some point."

"I think that's all the updates for now," Erica said. She checked her phone. "The guys are on their way back. Are you going to wait for Zach to go to dinner?"

"Yeah, we'll take separate cars in case Zach wants to go somewhere else later. I'm heading back to the cabin. See you soon." Autumn hugged Erica again, then left and crossed the clearing back to her cabin. She opened a couple of the windows and lay down on the couch to rest until Zach returned.

Deputy Reilly Brown pulled into the parking lot at the town park and stared at his cousin. He took in the hand-painted sign that Chase and his friends had been carrying down here every weekend for the last couple of months. Their message had never deterred any of the Bigfoot hunters that had made their way to Tahoma Valley, but he supposed that the young guys felt this was the only acceptable way to get their feelings across to tourists.

Chase had confessed that he and a couple of the others now sitting with him on the lawn had bought a cheap ape suit and had tried to scare some of the people who were chatting excitedly about Bigfoot while out on hikes in the area. Reilly had given his cousin a stern warning and told him to pass it along to his friends. That was a dangerous stunt. Anyone out on the trails could be carrying a gun, and a lot of people wouldn't hesitate to shoot what they thought was a monster in exchange for the fame it would bring them.

The message must have gotten through, because the ape suit had been dropped off at Reilly's home a couple of days later. The Bigfoot sightings hadn't stopped, though, and Reilly was concerned about that. Tahoma Valley had so much more going on than being the home to the Northwest's most famous cryptid. He didn't want his hometown to only be known for a monster.

He waved at Chase, took a few minutes to check out the park from the comfort of his truck's front seat, then pulled out again. The guys would take the sign down when the rangers came to close the park gate, and everything would be quiet again. Most of the guys there had jobs during the week, so the sign wouldn't be back up again until next Saturday.

He was concerned about the increasing number of campsite attacks at the campground. No people had been hurt so far. It seemed like whatever animal was causing the disturbances waited in the forest to make sure humans were out of sight. If it was Bigfoot, he knew that showed signs of a deeper intelligence than he had ever thought possible for the creature. Reilly had never had much of an interest in learning about what Bigfoot might supposedly really be, or its presumed intellect, but Carson had an extensive collection of books on the topic. Maybe he should borrow a few of them.

He drove to the medical clinic, which was next door to the Valley Tavern on the highway. The two buildings were separated by a quarter of a mile of a thick tree grove, so the clinic appeared to be in a remote setting. He loved the look of the log buildings along this part of the road. They had all been built in the forties, with some modifications done along the way as needed.

The clinic's yard was well-tended. Reilly got out of his car and stared at a shed at the far end of the property. It was mostly for storage, but there was a room underneath it that only a few people in town had ever known about. There had once been an entrance to the room, known to some people as the vault, in the shed, but Carson had closed off that door completely. He didn't want strangers to accidentally open it. The only entrance now was through the clinic.

Reilly entered the clinic and waved at the receptionist and security guard. "Doctor Smith in?" he asked.

"In his office," the receptionist replied. He headed past the front desk and down the hall. One exam room was occupied. The clinic had equipment for basic surgical procedures and was able to treat the common wounds and injuries that people sustained while hiking or camping. For anything far more serious, Carson and the other part-time doctors occasionally on duty would stabilize the patient and call for transportation to a larger city hospital. They were well aware of their limitations, and thankfully traumatic injuries were not often part of the practice.

Reilly found Carson in his office, standing at a door that was usually kept locked. "Going down or coming up?" Reilly asked quietly, closing the office door behind him.

"Coming up. The tested piece from the hair and skin sample Mitzi found was returned yesterday, so I put it on the counter next to Autumn's backpack."

"Do you think we should return that to her? Mitzi said she's coming back to town with Zach Larson today."

"Really? Crap." Carson finished locking the door and placed the key back into its hiding place. "No, there would be no point. Any of the blood still in those vials is not going to be useful. The stains on the pack will never come out. We might as well just keep it here."

"I agree."

"How are things out there?"

"Quiet." Reilly opened the door again. "How's your dad?"

"He's fine. Now that the fence is up along the highway, fewer people are trying to get down to the cave."

"Good. I better get back out on patrol."

Reilly waved at Carson, then left the clinic. He waited for a car to pass and thought about where to go next. He decided to take another drive through the campground. A car with a few people inside slowed down and turned into the lot for the tavern. He thought he recognized Autumn's friends. He forgot their names, but knew they were all interested in looking for Bigfoot. He was curious about why Zach would be coming out here, and decided to talk to him soon.

Reilly's phone rang, and he answered it. "Hi, Joey," he said. Joey Singleton was often his partner during a shift. Today they had been patrolling separately.

"Hi, Reilly. We have an incident over at the shopping center. Can you provide backup?"

"On my way." He sighed and turned to head back over to the strip mall. The campground and the creature lurking around it would have to wait.

CHAPTER 6

"No Bigfoot here!" Zach shouted out from the bathroom down the hall.

"No Bigfoot here," Autumn agreed with a laugh. Zach had returned about thirty minutes ago. Her friends had already left for the tavern, and she and Zach were getting changed for dinner. "I wonder how long they'll keep that up."

"Has anyone on the BOG forum mentioned it?"

Autumn finished brushing her hair and quickly put on a baseball-style tunic, buttoning it up and smoothing it out. "No, not that I can recall."

"Hey, I set up a trail camera at the back of this cabin," Zach called out. She heard him hang a towel back up on the rack. "You never know what might appear around here, or when."

"Good idea." She checked her purse to make sure her wallet and phone were inside.

"So, what was the work emergency about?" Zach asked, appearing in the bedroom doorway. He had taken a shower and changed into a dark green polo shirt and jeans. Autumn loved that color on him.

She told him about a mistake in the library's catalog as they left the cabin and got into his truck. "And of course, it couldn't wait until Monday, when I was already gone. But it's fixed, so I shouldn't hear from them until next week." Autumn had taken several vacation days for this trip out here, even though some of them would be spent relaxing back home.

"Well, now you can focus on why we're here." They chatted about Stan's purchase of the land near the cave and George's willingness for an interview. When they reached the Valley Tavern, they went inside and were greeted by a hostess who directed them to a booth already occupied by their friends. Zach and Autumn slid in to the last empty spaces.

"Mitzi and Marvin thought they saw something near one

of their dumpsters," Autumn told the group as they studied the paper menus. "And Zach said Mitzi found a strange hair and skin sample that she turned over the police. That's about all I know right now," she finished. She looked around the dining room. Only a few other tables were occupied.

Erica nudged her from across the table. "Have you said hi to Tony yet?" she asked with a grin.

Autumn rolled her eyes. She had seen Tony and his friends when they walked through the restaurant to their table. She had ignored a small hand wave from Aaron. Just knowing that they were here, and would probably be trying to interfere with her group's investigation, was irritating enough. She wasn't interested in sparking up a conversation with any of them.

Loud cheers resonated from the bar across the hall. "Must be a touchdown," Nate said to Mike. Bill checked his phone and nodded. "Third quarter," he told them.

"Football already?" Erica asked.

"Last pre-season game," Bill explained.

Zach looked at the menu. "I see they added a 'Bigfoot special'" he laughed. "Two half-pound burgers, two hot dogs, French fries, onion rings, and a bowl of salad. If one person eats it all, they get a free meal and a special Valley Tavern shirt."

"It's the salad that's really the challenge," Autumn laughed.

A waitress approached them. Zach recognized her instantly. "Hi, I'm Jessie. Can I get some drinks started for you?" She gave the group a closer look, and smiled at Zach. "Oh goodness! You're Zach Larson!"

"Yes," Zach replied modestly. "Hi, Jessie."

"You remember me?" she asked, sounding pleased.

"Yes. I spent a few hours with your boyfriend this afternoon."

"George," she said. "He probably tried to call me, but I've been busy most of the day. How long are you all in town?"

"A few days," Bill replied. "Has anyone ordered the new

Bigfoot special recently?"

"About once a week we get someone trying it out," Jessie said. "Only two people have succeeded so far. It's a lot of food."

"Sure is," Mike agreed. "I'd like a Coke, please."

The others placed their orders. As Jessie was about to walk away, Zach held up his hand. "Excuse me, Jessie. Would you have a few minutes to talk to me later?"

"Sure," she said. "I'm on until nine. Just let me know and I'll clear it with my boss, Troy."

"The bartender?"

"He's also now the owner," she said. "I'll get those drinks." She walked away.

"Do you think she has something to tell us?" Autumn asked.

"Maybe," Zach said. George had seemed eager for Zach to talk to Jessie.

He knew that once he started asking questions of people, his reason for being here in town wouldn't be a secret. He still wanted to keep it as quiet as possible. He had seen many instances where, once word spread that the show *Creature Hunt* was in town, complete strangers would show up at his hotel or wherever they saw the show's crew and try to get a completely made-up story on air. Zach always encouraged them to e-mail him, and he would contact them if he could accommodate their requests. It cut down on a lot of baseless claims when people realized they weren't instantly going to be on television because they thought they saw a monster.

Jessie returned with their drinks and took their food orders. "So, there was a bit of news from George that I wasn't expecting," he told the group. He had informed them that Stan had given them permission to head onto his property as long as they let him know they were there. "He thinks he saw a Bigfoot body."

"A dead Bigfoot?" Bill shouted. People at three other tables turned to look at them, and Autumn blushed. She saw Tony gazing at her with a look of contempt, and she glared back at him.

"Shhh," Erica hissed.

"A body?" Mike echoed quietly.

"Yes. He saw it once, and it was gone by the time he returned to look for it again. He thinks there's only one Bigfoot still down at the cave. Maybe the younger creature moved on to another part of the area, and this older one is now simply trying to survive and defend its territory. And it's backed up by another guy I spoke to. One of the men near the Bigfoot sign at the park brought it up first. He also saw the body and thinks it had been attacked by another animal."

Everyone stared at each other, wondering what kind of animal in the area would take on a Bigfoot. "A fight for dominance?" Mike suggested.

"If we're right about a Bigfoot family, it was probably the female that died," Nate said.

Zach nodded. "I think the female Bigfoot was killed by something looking for food."

Erica had been quietly looking around the dining room. She got up from her end of the booth. Autumn watched as Erica pulled out her cell phone and turned on the camera. She stood and walked over to a wall that advertised the Bigfoot Burger special promotion and took some pictures, then appeared to casually take some other pictures around the dining room. She slid back into the booth and showed Autumn a picture of Tony and his group. "Those guys over there are plotting something for sure," she said, showing everyone at the table. They all looked up and saw Aaron folding what appeared to be some sort of map and placing it into his backpack as their food arrived. "We should keep an eye on them."

Talia looked around Tony and thought she recognized the man at the booth across the dining room. "Should I know that guy?" she asked. "He looks familiar."

Aaron smiled. "Have you heard of the show *Creature Hunt*?"

She nodded. A couple of her friends were really into the reality television show. "It's kind of similar to what you guys are doing, right?"

"Something like that," Tony agreed. "Anyway, the guy over there is the host, Zach Larson. The woman sitting next to him is his girlfriend, Autumn Hunter." Tony shook his head. "She's obsessed with Bigfoot. More so than we are. She and her friends are probably here to see where we investigate, then take over and try to copy what we've been doing."

Talia thought he was being overly dramatic. She had treated herself to a nice day, finding a salon in town and getting both a manicure and a pedicure. A stop at the ice cream parlor and the candy store had satisfied her appetite and allowed her to pick up some candy she hadn't seen in years. She had finally spent some time in the hot tub, and then driven to a park in town to do some people watching before meeting up with Tony and his friends. She was finding them to be very single-minded and not very interesting this evening. She was also wondering why Aaron and Cal had just been studying a map of the town's medical clinic.

She was relieved when the waitress returned and placed her cheeseburger and fries in front of her. They had all ordered variations of the same dish. "So, Talia, we were wondering if you could help us out with something."

"What is it?" she asked.

"I was kind of hoping that you would distract Zach and his friends tomorrow night while we go someplace to look for evidence of Bigfoot," Tony said before taking a large bite of his burger.

Talia focused on her own food for a full minute as thoughts ran through her head. "Why would you want me to do that?" she asked quietly. Cal's eyes were focused intently on her as she took a sip of her water.

"Because we're looking in a place they've been to before, and we'd like to keep Zach away from there," Tony said. "It will be easy, I promise. He and his girlfriend are trying to get some pictures of Bigfoot, and maybe even the same type of physical samples we're looking for. They'll definitely want to hear another Bigfoot story, and it will help us with our research."

Talia thought of all the times her recent ex-boyfriend had promised her something and not followed through on the promise. "What are you offering me?" she asked. If she was going to get caught up in a scheme to help these guys, she decided on the spot that she was going to be rewarded for it in some way.

"Five hundred dollars," Tony said. He pulled that amount out of his pocket and placed it on the table. Aaron and Cal started coughing. Across the room, Talia saw the woman Tony had called Autumn looking their way. She shrank back against the seat.

"Tony, that's way over the top," Aaron hissed. Cal glared at him.

"Five hundred," Tony repeated, pushing the money over to Talia's hand. His eyes stared right into hers. "Just to tell someone a small lie. Heck, it's not even quite a lie. You've already seen a monster, or thought you did. I just need you to recall how you felt last night, while making up an encounter with a Bigfoot."

"Will you tell me what I need to say?" Talia asked. "Write down what I'm supposed to have seen and I'll do it. I'll make it believable enough that he'd want to use it on his show."

Tony smiled. "We can do that. I'll bring over a copy of a story tomorrow morning. We'll need you to go over to Cabin One at the resort around seven o'clock tomorrow night. We'll handle the rest ourselves."

Talia nodded. She was usually always honest, sometimes to a fault. It might be fun to go over to Zach Larson and try to convince him that she had seen Bigfoot. It was unlikely that she'd ever see him or his group over there again. She already knew that she was planning to never see Tony again after this week.

Her initial attraction to him had faded over the course of the day as she had focused on herself. She had only kept her promise to have dinner with them out of curiosity, and now she'd agreed to do a favor for them in exchange for money. It was a business deal, no more than that, and she found the opportunity to step out of her comfort zone a little exciting. She slid the bills into her purse and continued eating.

With that matter settled, Tony sat back and enjoyed the rest of his dinner. After some silence, Aaron and Cal finished their meals, as well. "Are we sure this is going to stop Zach from going to the cave?" Cal finally said. "I mean, what if he has already been down there?"

"We'll deal with that later," Tony said. "And when we go to the clinic after the cave..."

"What clinic?" Talia asked brightly. Her eyes strayed to the floor plans sticking out of a bag.

Aaron glared at Tony. "We have an interview scheduled with someone at the local medical clinic," he said. "They asked to meet with us late at night because they're usually busier during the day."

Talia smiled. She had a feeling they were lying to her, but she didn't care. She had her money. After she went to Zach with her Bigfoot story, she'd stick around for a couple of days and enjoy the rest of her impromptu vacation.

"Thank you for dinner," she said, placing some cash on the table. "It's getting late. I'll see you tomorrow, around ten?"

"Fine," Tony said. He slid out and let her leave. Once they were alone, Cal's eyes narrowed.

"Are you insane?" he asked. "Five hundred dollars just to distract Zach and Autumn for a couple of hours?"

Tony shrugged. "We bought her loyalty for a bit. I'm fine with that. She'll tell them the story, we'll have some time to look around near the cave without being bothered, and then we'll figure out a reason to show up at the clinic."

"At least I don't have to do it, now," Aaron grinned. The plan had originally involved him trying to convince Zach and

Autumn that he had a genuine Bigfoot sighting to share. He was happy that he'd get to go along with his friends tomorrow night.

"Fine," Cal grumbled. They paid the waitress and left the tavern.

On their way out, they noticed that Zach and Autumn's friends had left, and the couple had lingered at their table, chatting with one of the men they had seen behind the bar when they had entered. Tony wondered why Zach would still be here, but his mind was soon taken over by the plans for the next evening. He was sure that this time, he would return from Tahoma Valley with proof that monsters lurked here.

CHAPTER 7

Zach and Autumn moved to the bar, where they both ordered sodas and watched a football game until they saw Jessie enter the room. She had removed her apron and had a purse with her. Zach checked his watch and saw it was only half past eight.

"Hi!" Jessie said brightly as she slid into the booth across from Zach and Autumn. She released her hair from a ponytail and shook it out. "It's slow, so Troy said I could take off a few minutes early." Troy, once again standing behind the bar, looked over at them and said something to another waitress.

"Hi, Jessie. Thanks for agreeing to talk to us," Autumn said. The waitress delivered another tray of sodas, with one for Jessie, and told them to let her know if they needed anything else. Zach thanked her and placed a twenty-dollar bill on the tray. That earned him a wide smile as the waitress headed back to the bar.

"You were nice about asking. Not like some of the other guests I've served this summer." Jessie shook her head. "Whenever we get a big crowd of Bigfoot hunters, people just seem to think that all the local people owe them information."

"Do you mind if we record this?" Zach asked. "I might be able to use some of your information in an episode of *Creature Hunt*."

"Sure," Jessie agreed. Zach gave Autumn his phone to use. He was grateful that the bar was not very busy, and that Troy had pointed them to a booth in the back of the lounge, away from other patrons.

"Thank you." Autumn started the video camera and asked Jessie for her name, then sat back to let Zach speak while she kept the camera steady.

"I'm going to start with a direct question. Have you ever seen Bigfoot?"

"I don't think so," she replied. "Not that I could say with certainty. But my boyfriend, George, insists that one comes up to his house and looks in the window."

"He's still seeing that?" Autumn asked in surprise. Jessie raised her eyebrows. "Sorry. He told us a couple of years ago that he thought a Bigfoot was looking in his windows."

Jessie nodded. "Yeah. I think he's just accepted it now. He sent a text a few minutes ago to let me know that Zach is interviewing him on camera tomorrow."

Zach nodded. "Have you observed any creatures looking into his house?"

"One night back in March, I stayed over because it was snowing hard. When he got up to use the bathroom while we were watching a movie, I went to the kitchen." She paused, clasping her hands together. "There was an outline of a tall, wide animal at the back door. It was definitely not a human, and not a bear. I turned on the light, and whatever it was, it ran off on two legs. I told George about it and he ran to the door to see if anything was out in the yard." She shrugged. "Nothing was there."

"Did anything else happen that night?"

"No. The next morning, there were large tracks near the front porch, but they were almost filled in with fresh snow."

Autumn shivered. She had believed that a Bigfoot had found her house after her first trip to Tahoma Valley. The sightings had disappeared within a few months, and she had managed to convince herself that they were all in her imagination. She wondered how often that happened to other people who had an encounter with a monster.

"Before we go any further, did George tell you about the campground last night?" Jessie asked.

Zach thought back to the afternoon's conversation. "No. What about it?"

"Something's been trashing campsites and scaring people over there. So far, it's been kept pretty quiet. We went to Rainier Lake yesterday, and as we were leaving, we passed a camper that had huge dents and a couple of torn window screens. There was also a broken cooler in the bed of the truck."

"Really? I'll have to look into that," Zach said. Autumn nodded. Zach watched Jessie as she played with her straw wrapper, winding it through her fingers repeatedly.

"George mentioned that you had an encounter with another creature," Zach said softly. "Are you sure this wasn't a bear encounter?"

"Do bears growl like a dog?" Jessie asked.

Zach blinked. "Not that I know of," he said. "Please, tell us what happened."

"I was just getting off of a shift. It was late afternoon. Troy asked me to take out a bag of trash before I left. I propped the door open and could smell the kitchen, particularly the hamburgers that the cooks had been making all day. I reached the dumpster, threw the bag in, and then heard a low growl."

Her voice caught, and Zach saw real fear in her eyes. "I've never heard a sound like that, even from my dad's dog. This was low, and guttural, and every hair on my body stood up." She bit her lip. "It wasn't quite dark yet. I started to walk back to the kitchen, then turned around. I saw a tall figure, probably about seven feet tall. It had a body like a wolf on steroids, and it was standing on its hind legs. It had bright yellow eyes. That's what always stands out the most in my mind. The eyes."

She shook her head as if clearing the image from her brain. "It was too…canine-like to be a Bigfoot, at least from what I've heard. I've never known a wolf to be that big, or stand on two legs for any length of time. It wasn't holding on to anything, because I could see its hands."

"Hands?" Zach echoed. Autumn's heart was racing, and she struggled to keep the camera steady.

"Yes. Paws, but it also had long fingers that ended in claws. I don't know how long I stood there, but I finally heard Troy calling to me. The creature snapped its jaws at me, then walked into the forest. Walked. On two legs." She shook her head. "It then dropped down out of sight, and I could see the bushes moving as it crept away."

"What color was it?" Zach asked.

"Its hair was brown." Jessie drank from her soda. "I called George to come and get me, and I didn't leave until he pulled up right in front of the door. Any time since then that Troy's asked me to go out there, I ask someone to stand at the door."

"Did you tell any of the other staff here about your encounter?"

"Only Troy. I didn't want anyone else to get scared. I haven't seen that thing since that night."

"When was this sighting?" Autumn asked.

"In June."

She nodded. That was around the time that an influx of Bigfoot sightings had started flowing to the BOG forum. Something else in the woods was forcing the Bigfoot to come out into the open, making it more visible to anyone looking for it.

"Thank you for telling us, Jessie," Zach said gently. Autumn shut off the phone and grabbed her soda, suddenly very thirsty.

"Do you know what I saw?" Jessie asked. "You must have come across something like this on your show. Have other people seen wolves walking on two legs?"

"Are you sure you want to know?" Autumn asked. Jessie nodded eagerly, and Zach sighed.

"I've already come across a couple of signs that one was here. What you saw, Jessie, is frequently referred to in cryptid circles as an upright canine, or a dogman."

"Dogman," she repeated. "Yeah, that's actually a pretty good description. Have you seen one?"

"Yes," Zach said. "Autumn and I have both had dogman encounters. There have also been a couple of episodes on the show about them."

"I'll have to go and watch them," Jessie said. "It's actually sort of a relief to put a name to it." She looked around. "I still am not sure if I want a lot of people to know about it."

"That's understandable. They won't hear anything from

us unless you approve something we want to use in the show."

"That's all I can tell you," she said, finishing her soda. "I need to get home."

"Thank you," Autumn said.

"I hope we'll see you again before we leave town," Zach added. Jessie got up and walked away, automatically taking their empty glasses and placing them on the bar as she left the tavern.

"A dogman?" Autumn asked in a quiet, tense voice. "When did you see one here?"

"Signs of one," he reminded her, placing the phone back in his coat pocket. "When I was down by the cave earlier with George and Stan. I didn't have a chance to say anything before dinner."

"Does this change why we're here?" she asked.

"No," he said firmly. "We're here to look for evidence of Bigfoot that we can bring to the show. If there's a dogman here, maybe we'll get lucky and get evidence of that, too."

"Okay," she replied. "Can we go now? I'm tired."

He nodded, and they left the tavern. Out here, closer to the mountain, the nights were already getting cool, and she leaned close to Zach's warmth as they headed for his truck. They were grateful for an uneventful ride back to the cabin, and both of them fell asleep quickly.

CHAPTER 8

George arrived at the cabin shortly before ten o'clock the next morning. Autumn went out to the porch to greet him and saw a dark-colored sedan approaching the clearing. As soon as she looked at it, the driver, shielded by shade from the evergreen trees on either side of the path, stopped driving. The car began to back up slowly, then paused.

Autumn's attention turned back to George. She was surprised to also see Stan getting out of the truck. He waved at her as he came around the front of the vehicle and stood beside George. "Hi, Autumn! I figured I might as well come along. Zach wanted to talk to me, too."

George turned around and saw the vehicle that had caught Autumn's attention. It rolled out of sight. "I saw that car at the general store on my way in."

She shrugged. "Probably a wrong turn." She smiled at George and Stan and shook their hands. "It's good to see both of you. George, thank you for agreeing to tell us your story again."

George nodded. He had spoken with Jessie last night, after her shift, expressing some doubts about releasing his Bigfoot story to the world. She had encouraged him to talk to Zach and see how the interview progressed. "Zach's got a good head on his shoulders," she had pointed out. "He's not out to exploit anyone. He's just looking for what people believe to be the truth."

Emboldened by his girlfriend's courage at telling her own story, he had agreed. Now, in the broad daylight and warm sunshine, his nervousness the night before seemed silly. Having his dad beside him, someone who knew he wasn't crazy when he mentioned Bigfoot, was also a comfort. They followed Autumn into the cabin.

Zach had set up a camera on a tripod and his laptop was on the coffee table. He had re-arranged a couple of the chairs so that George would be sitting against the wall with nothing distracting in the background. A patchwork quilt, green and cream with a tree embroidered in the middle, was the only piece of decoration beyond the lamp.

"Hi, George," Zach said, and welcomed the other man with a hug. "Stan! Thanks for coming along. That will save us a trip. Would you like something to drink?"

"Just water," George said. Stan agreed. Autumn retrieved bottles while Zach gestured for George to settle into the chair and then sat down again himself.

"Stan, if you'll just sit over there on the couch while I interview George, I'd appreciate it," Zach said. "When we're done talking, I'll ask you some questions as well."

"No problem," Stan said. Autumn handed everyone their water, then took a seat on the couch, close to Stan and near the front window, where she could see if anyone was heading their way and quietly take care of any random visitors herself.

Zach made sure the cameras were on, then introduced himself. "I'm here with George Smith, a resident of the town of Tahoma Valley. Twelve years ago, George and a friend had an encounter with a Sasquatch that ended in tragedy. George has agreed to tell his story."

George remained silent. "I'm not sure where to start," he admitted, taking a sip of his water.

"That's okay. I'll ask some questions to get you started. Where did this encounter take place?"

"Near a cave on the edge of town, close to my dad's house. Back then it was public property and the town had listed the cave on local maps so tourists could have another place to explore."

Autumn observed Stan's reactions to Zach's questions. He seemed interested in the cameras and the voice recorders. A couple of times he looked as though he wanted to interrupt, but stilled himself. Autumn smiled at him and they quietly listened to George speak.

Zach continued to guide George with questions. An hour later, the story of his friend's fatal encounter with Bigfoot had emerged, and George's emotions were obvious. "I'm telling this as a counterpoint to all the 'Let's go see if Bigfoot really is dangerous' stories that I've seen online since my experience," he explained. "The monster killed my friend. I've had a few encounters since then, mostly at night around my house or if I've been fishing and the fish are still in my truck."

Zach nodded. "And do you still go down to the cave?"

"As little as possible. I don't know that the Bigfoot still lives there, and I don't want to know for sure. There are signs that it's still in the area. My dad owns the land now and calls the police when trespassers make trouble down there."

Zach asked a few more questions. Autumn listened carefully to the whole interview. It was very much the same story he had told them two years ago, which made it even more believable in her eyes. Stan frowned at the part about George finding the Bigfoot body and simply leaving it behind, but she found nothing odd about it. He had been nervous about reporting it, and it was an understandable reaction.

She saw Nate and Mike step out from Cabin Two and look in her direction. She waved her phone at them, and a moment later received a text message.

Is Zach available?
No. Doing an interview.
We're heading across the creek to look around.
I'll let him know.

Zach stood and turned off the cameras. Stan also stood and stretched. George looked at the clock on the wall and blinked. "That went by fast. How much of all of that is going to be on the show?"

"I'm not sure yet. It depends on how many other people I talk to, and what video and pictures I can get to support what people are talking about." Zach smiled. "Jessie spoke to us last night, and I'm hoping we can use some of that footage."

"Oh, she mentioned that the campground has had a few incidents," Autumn said casually.

George nodded. "Yeah, the police were there the other

night to look at a camper that got trashed."

"Fourth time this summer," Stan noted. "I bet they left food out."

Zach laughed. "Isn't that usually how animals get attracted to human places?" He took a moment to reset his equipment. "Stan, it's your turn."

"I need to walk around for a bit," George said. "I'm going to head over to the general store. I'll be back."

"Okay," Zach said. When George left, Autumn got straight to the point.

"You didn't like George's story about finding a dead Bigfoot," she said to Stan as he got comfortable in the chair across from Zach.

"That's right. He should have at least reported it to the police."

"He's not the only one who saw it," Zach said. "I spoke to a young man named Chase Brown who told me about it."

"Hmmm," Stan replied. "Reilly Brown's cousin. Maybe that body didn't entirely decompose, after all."

Zach stood still for a moment, shocked that he hadn't already made the connection. If Reilly knew about the Bigfoot's body, maybe part of it had made it down into the vault that was supposedly somewhere in town. Rumors had been swirling for awhile that people in Tahoma Valley kept secret evidence of Bigfoot hidden away from the public, hoping to make stories disappear. He was now even more determined to get into the vault, and knew who he'd have to talk to in order to make it work.

Two hours later, George and Stan left. "Now, don't forget that your friends are welcome to come by my place any time," Stan reminded Autumn. She nodded and said that she would pass along the message. Stan's interview had been full of stories from around the area, about seeing Bigfoot and a few times that people had pulled pranks that made someone think they were seeing the monster. Autumn figured Zach wanted some personal anecdotes to fill in what life around the town was usually like, and Stan was full of history. This episode was not meant to focus only on Bigfoot, but also on its importance to the people of the town.

70

CHAPTER 9

It was already early afternoon. Autumn and Zach set up his laptop on the kitchen table to see if there were any interesting pictures from the cameras. They only saw George and Stan leaving the road, and some deer and smaller forest animals.

Autumn brought out some snacks. "Nate and Mike went to the other side of the creek a couple of hours ago," she told him as they ate. She had seen them walk past the cabin shortly after the text exchange. Erica had not been with them, and Autumn figured she was probably enjoying some quiet time over in the cabin.

Autumn went upstairs to take a short nap, and Zach walked around the back of the cabin to think about the interviews. He knew it had been a tough story for George to tell. He was also still thinking about the dead Bigfoot, and wondering why the dogman had attacked the other creature.

He sat on the boulder and stared across the creek. He could occasionally hear voices coming from the forest on the opposite side, and knew people were over there on the hiking trails. Autumn's friends were probably still over there, though not visible to him at the moment. He wasn't sure how long he was sitting on the rock before a sound finally brought him out of his daze.

"Zach!" a voice called. He turned and saw Reilly walking his way.

"Deputy Brown," he greeted the other man, who sat on another large rock a few feet away. "I was just thinking about the shelter that used to be over there."

Reilly smiled. "I'm happy to say it hasn't returned. It worried us, Zach. Carson and I knew it meant that one of the creatures was marking its territory up here, and we had hoped they'd stay in the cave."

"Perhaps after I cut off one of their family member's hands, they tried to stay away from humans."

Reilly nodded, his gaze sharp as Nate, Mike, and Bill came into view over at the clearing. They had cameras and appeared to be looking around at the ground, and then over at the water. "Seems like they have. Sightings have been scarce since then, at least any that have been reported to us. Then June came along, and the reports flooded in to our office."

"Why do you think they've suddenly started up again this summer?"

Reilly shrugged. "I've heard you've already spoken to George and Stan. And Jessie. Didn't they have any ideas?"

"No."

Reilly looked around. "Keep this between us for now. My cousin, Chase, and his friends were dressing in an ape suit and scaring people around that time. They stopped. Sightings continued." He shrugged again.

"I met Chase yesterday. He said he saw a dead Bigfoot."

"He told you that?"

"Yes. Is it true?"

Reilly looked him in the eyes. "By the time I heard about it, and went to check it out, I just found scattered bones."

"Where are they now?"

Reilly pulled out his phone and started to type something. Zach watched the men kneel to look at something at the edge of the trees. They took pictures of it and, seeing Zach and Reilly on the opposite side of the creek, waved and disappeared further down the trail. Once they were out of sight, Zach stood and crossed the creek using a couple of stones jutting up from the ground. Reilly put away the phone, sighed, and then joined him.

The two men crouched down and looked at a large footprint. It was not the usual over-sized humanoid print that Zach was used to seeing with Bigfoot. This was thinner and looked more like an over-sized wolf print. Reilly whistled and placed his hand next to it. "What kind of animal do you think made that?"

Zach pulled out his phone and took a couple of pictures. "I have a guess. If you want to know more, you're going to have to show me the vault."

Reilly stood. "What vault?"

Zach faced him. "You know exactly what I'm talking about. The place where you put all the evidence you find of Bigfoot. The place you and Carson Smith have kept secret from almost the whole town."

"It's going to stay a secret."

"I'm not going to argue with that. I just want to see what's there, and what people have left behind or given up to you over the years. Or had taken from them."

Reilly flinched. "Still not over the photos being taken from your camera?"

"I don't want it to happen again."

Reilly looked around them, as if to make sure no one was standing nearby to overhear them. "I'm going to need to ask Carson about your request."

"Better do it quick. I want to see it tomorrow."

"Why the rush?"

"I'm only going to be in town for a few days." He decided to take the leap. "Do you have a dead Bigfoot in there?"

"Not a whole one, no," Reilly shot back. Zach stared at him, and Reilly's face turned red. "I mean, we do have the hand that you chopped off the Bigfoot a couple of years ago."

"So, we're way past the 'what vault' stage, aren't we?"

Reilly cursed and looked away. Zach waited him out. Finally, the deputy nodded. "I'll get back to you later with a response, after I talk to Carson," Reilly promised. "What are your plans for tonight?"

"We're going to monitor the cameras. Hopefully, we can go take them down tomorrow night and then put together enough footage for a complete episode of *Creature Hunt*."

"Is that why you're really here?" Reilly asked casually as they stepped back across the creek.

"Yes. You can ask anyone I've talked to so far if you have doubts. I did get a hint that I should ask around at the campground to learn what people have seen over there."

"Or think they've seen." Reilly's gaze was intense.

Zach nodded. "Yeah, there's always that issue. People who are looking for monsters tend to think everything they find is pointing to that creature."

Zach walked Reilly to his car, parked in front of the house. To his surprise, Joey was also there. "Hi, Deputy Singleton," he said.

"Zach, you know you can call me Joey."

He smiled at her. "Reilly didn't tell me you were waiting for him."

"That's okay. I had a nice chat with the women over at Cabin Two." Zach looked over and saw Erica and Autumn on the porch, sitting in camp chairs.

"We better get going," Reilly said. "We have some patrolling to do in town." The deputies drove away, and Zach went over to Cabin Two. The guys returned from their explorations just as Zach sat down. They were excited about the prints they had seen.

"Anything interesting show up yet?" he asked Erica, who had been watching the camera monitors for the past few hours.

"Nope. There was only one car that showed up other than a sheriff vehicle going past Stan's house. I thought it looked like Tony's car, but I can't be sure."

"Hey," Autumn said. "A car I didn't recognize showed up here just after George arrived this morning. The driver slowed down, saw us, then backed up down the road."

Zach thought about the car, but his mind kept pushing it away and bringing the pawprint into his brain. He blinked his eyes. "Okay. I think I need some quiet time here. Let's get an early dinner."

Mike and Nate drove into town to pick up sandwiches, and the group ate together at Cabin Two. By the time Zach retreated to his cabin, it was already starting to get dark in their part of the resort. "I'll be watching the cameras," he told Autumn. "If something really urgent comes up, let me know. Otherwise, I could use some time to myself."

She nodded in understanding. Although Zach was very outgoing, there were times when he preferred solitude to think, or to put together whatever project he was working on.

She was often the same way, and it helped that their house had plenty of space for them to each have a private work area. Here, though, she knew he would prefer to have the whole cabin to himself for a couple of hours.

"I'll stay here, and be back over around nine," she told him, and he kissed her. He left, and she sat down on the couch to chat with Erica and look at videos on her phone.

"I'm kind of restless," Mike admitted after a few minutes of watching the camera images. "You know what? I'm going to go over to Stan's house."

"I'll go with you," Nate offered.

"Hey, guys, wait," Autumn said. She looked over at her cabin. "Zach really wanted us to stay away from the cave."

"Stan told Zach we were welcome any time," Mike pointed out. "I just want to go over there for a couple of hours. If nothing happens, we'll come back. I promise, we won't go down to the cave unless we see something on camera that we can check out."

"I can't stop you," Autumn admitted.

"Be careful," Erica warned. Mike and Nate promised they would be safe, and then left. Erica took their place at the computer and Autumn sat next to her.

"Well, this is interesting," Bill said. He was looking out the front window of the cabin from the recliner on the other side of the living room.

Autumn looked out the window as a gray car pulled up in front of Cabin Two. She realized that it was the same car that had driven down the road to their cabins earlier that day. A tall, slim woman got out and looked around, her gaze resting on Cabin One before switching to Cabin Two. "Who's this?" she muttered as the woman closed the car door and walked up to the porch. Her long black hair whipped around in the evening breeze, and pale skin seemed to make her face glow in the dim light.

The woman knocked on the door. Bill answered, having been watching from behind Autumn. "Hello," he said. "Can we help you?" Erica moved into the doorway as well, while Autumn stayed at the table, looking at the monitors.

"Is this where I can find Zach Larson?" the woman asked in a low, nervous voice. She glanced behind her, then turned to face the door again. "Mitzi pointed me in this direction. I have something I need to talk to him about."

Erica pulled back from the door. "Please, come in."

"Is Zach in there?"

Annoyed, Autumn stood and marched over to the door. She looked directly at the woman. "What is it you need to talk to him about?"

The woman took a step back. "He's the monster guy, right? I heard he was in town this weekend, and I think…I think I've seen a Bigfoot."

"Join the club," Bill muttered. Erica glared at him. Autumn stepped out onto the porch with the woman.

"Come with me over to the other cabin. I'm his girlfriend, and you can talk about anything you want with both of us."

The woman looked over at the other cabin. "Thank you. I'm Talia, by the way."

"I'm Autumn. Come on over." She looked back at the others. "Text or call if you need anything. You know what to look for."

Erica nodded in understanding. Autumn led Talia across the clearing. "When did this encounter happen?"

"Just this afternoon. I was driving through town and stopped for directions at a tavern. When I came out, I walked to my car, at the edge of the parking lot, and then…" her voice trailed off, and she seemed lost in thought.

Autumn opened the front door of the cabin. "Zach? There's someone here who'd like to talk to you." The room was still dimly lit, so she turned on an extra lamp on the end table.

Zach looked up from his laptop. Luckily, the screen was out of sight of anyone coming in the door. He just received a message from Erica about Autumn and the mysterious woman, so he smiled and stood up. "Hi, I'm Zach Larson," he said, shaking her hand. She smiled nervously and looked around. "Please, have a seat."

"Thanks," she said, and sat down on the couch. She peered out the window behind her, then turned to face him. Autumn took Zach's spot at the kitchen table. From this vantage point, she could see the living room and through the window. They had left the curtains open here, just like at the other cabin, until bedtime so that any creature, or person, approaching the cabin would be visible.

"What's your name?" Zach asked.

"Talia Harrison."

"May I record this conversation, Talia?"

"If you need to," she said quietly. He nodded and set up a voice recorder, then opened his notebook and noted the date, time, and Talia's name.

"Talia was just starting to tell me that she thinks she saw Bigfoot this afternoon," Autumn said, and Zach turned around. He smiled, but she nodded at the serious look that immediately came to his face. She sat back in the chair, watching for any motion on the cameras. One of them flashed, and she got a text from Bill asking if she had seen anything. She answered in the negative, then waited to hear the rest of Talia's story.

"As I was telling Autumn, I stopped at the tavern in town to ask for directions. My car was at the edge of the parking lot. When I came out of the building, I walked over to the car and immediately smelled something bad. I thought maybe there was a dumpster nearby. Then I noticed that there was something standing next to a tree, about fifty feet away from the lot."

"What did you see?" Zach asked, quietly taking notes. As Talia closed her eyes, he drew a quick sketch of the tavern parking lot, recalling that there was a thick stand of trees between the tavern and the clinic next door.

"It was just sort of a shape, really," she recalled, her eyes still closed. "I saw part of a tall, muscular body with long brownish hair. The head was kind of pointed, and there was a large hand on the tree trunk."

"A hand?" Zach repeated.

"Yes, a hand. It had human-looking fingers, but much larger than any I've ever seen. It was probably close to eight or nine feet tall."

"Any guess as to weight?"

She shook her head and opened her eyes. "No, I couldn't see enough of it. What really grabbed my attention was the one eye that I saw looking at me when the creature shifted position. It really seemed almost human, yet wild at the same time. Then, I heard someone calling out and whatever it was disappeared into the trees."

"What direction did it go in?"

"Towards the clinic."

"You know where the clinic is?" Zach asked smoothly.

Talia hesitated. "I passed by it a couple of days ago."

Autumn lowered her head and frowned. Why would Talia have needed to stop to ask for directions if she had already been here for a couple of days? She thought Zach might be wondering that, too, but he didn't ask Talia about it. Instead, he shifted the conversation.

"What made you think that the animal you saw was a Bigfoot?" he asked.

"I've read some stories here and there about people thinking they've seen one," she replied. "I never expected one of those people would be me." Her face flushed. "Do you really think there's one around here?"

Zach sat back and pretended to think about her question. He had the feeling that she wasn't telling him the complete truth. "There's probably a good chance of that."

Autumn looked at the message that had just popped up on Zach's computer. It was from Bill. He had attached a picture that Erica had taken at the Valley Tavern the night before, when they had all been having dinner there. *Check this out*, he typed. Autumn clicked on the photo.

She recognized Tony Simons and his friends, sitting in the

corner booth opposite from her group. She looked more closely and saw a woman with long black hair and a pale face next to Tony. While she couldn't be absolutely sure that it was Talia from the photo, it looked enough like her to cause a rush of anger in Autumn.

This is Autumn, she typed back. *Her name is Talia Harrison. She's talking to Zach right now, but I think she's making everything up.*

Call Mitzi. See if she really sent Talia here.

Can Erica call? I think I see something on the video.

Autumn turned her attention away from the messages and stared at the monitors. The trail cam at the parking lot had taken three photos, and they were slowly coming up. At the same time, she caught some movement on the video camera across from the cave.

Zach was asking Talia a few more questions, but Autumn lost interest in their conversation. She saw a tall shape standing at the mouth of the cave, and then three humans came into view and stopped walking. She recognized the people who appeared at the edge of the video. The humans stopped and stared at the cave.

Another message came through. *Mitzi didn't send anyone our way. She said she would never reveal that Zach was staying here to anyone other than people she knew or the sheriff.*

Knowing the camera would keep recording, Autumn stood and walked over to the living room. "Talia? Can I ask you a question?"

"Sure," Talia said, standing up and looking startled at the tone in Autumn's voice. She started to inch towards the door, but Zach caught on that something was wrong and moved quickly enough to reach the door before the woman could get there.

"How long have you known Tony Simons, and why did he send you here tonight?"

CHAPTER 10

"Someone lives down here?" Aaron asked as Tony drove down Forest Hill Road. A log cabin was set back from the road, and three people sat out in the front yard.

"Some old man," Tony said. "I saw him when I drove down here earlier to make sure this was the right place."

"You know we're trespassing, right?" Cal said. "You saw all those signs."

"We're not bothering anyone, and we're not partying or hunting. We're just here to see if we can find anything in the cave."

"Why not just go straight to the clinic, again?" Aaron asked as Tony pulled into an empty parking spot and shut off the engine.

"Because anything we can get straight from an animal will be better to test," Tony reminded him. "Come on, you should know that by now."

They got out of the car. Tony carried nothing but a camera and a flashlight. Cal placed a knife in his pocket. Aaron took the other flashlight and took the car keys from Tony. "If something happens, I'm running back out here to wait for you," he said.

Tony rolled his eyes and set out down the trail. "I don't think we should be here," Cal muttered as he and Aaron fell into line behind Tony. Although the moon was nearly full, it was darker here under the trees than back in the parking lot. He was still questioning the need to go to the cave when they already had a plan to steal some possible evidence from the clinic later tonight.

"This is where Zach and Autumn had their encounter a couple of years ago. It makes sense that the Bigfoot would still be here," Tony said. He walked steadily, keeping his flashlight pointed at the ground.

"Those people at the house we passed have probably called the sheriff," Aaron said. The three people sitting in the yard had looked up from the fire pit when they had passed.

Although Tony had driven as quickly as he could, Aaron thought he had recognized two people from Autumn Hunter's group.

A squirrel scrambling up a nearby tree made him jump. He looked up at the tree and saw the camera strapped to it. A red light was showing, which meant they were being recorded. He opened his mouth to say something and almost ran into Tony, who had stopped and turned off the flashlight.

"I knew it was here," Tony breathed. They could see a cave off to their left side. On the right-hand side, a path led up into the forest. The cave entrance was almost perfectly round, and through the darkness Tony thought he saw a flickering light inside. It could be a fire, and that got him excited about the possibilities of Bigfoot being here.

"What now?" Cal asked. He was becoming irritated with Tony, and nervous about how quiet the woods were. He no longer heard any of the usual insect sounds that had accompanied them on their walk to this clearing.

Aaron noticed it, too. He turned on his flashlight and aimed it at the trail cam. The red light was still glowing. "I think Zach was already down here," he said. Tony turned to the camera. "Someone's watching us," Aaron whispered.

You mean something," Cal replied. His voice shook as he saw a pair of glowing yellow eyes observing him from the trees about twenty feet away. At first, the eyes seemed to be floating just above the ferns, but as the creature rose into a standing position, the eyes reached a little over six feet into the air. They could hear bushes shaking as the creature moved.

Tony turned and swung his light over by the trees. All three men were shocked to discover what appeared to be a wolf standing on its hind legs. It bared its teeth and pushed tree branches aside with paws that looked eerily human, with long fingers and sharp claws.

Cal took a step back. "What the hell is that?" he asked. He was familiar with what Bigfoot was supposed to look like. He read almost everything he could about the ape-like creature, but he knew very little about other monsters.

"A dogman," Aaron answered. "Talia told us about it the other night, remember?" He had heard stories about such a thing, but until this weekend, he had never heard of one in Washington. As if sensing that the humans were interested in it, the creature swiftly disappeared behind the tree. A mournful, chilling howl emanated through the air, and Aaron felt his body start shaking.

An ear-splitting roar made them turn around to the cave. Tony's light fell on an enormous hairy body. It was dark brown, with eyes that seemed to glow red in the dark. Tony saw that something was wrong with one of its arms. It ended in a stump rather than the alarmingly large hand on the other arm. It opened its mouth to roar again, and the dogman stepped out into the clearing.

Aaron suddenly realized that the three men were in-between the two monsters, who were both displaying aggressive behavior. "It's time to go," he said. Cal nodded, and the two men started to retreat down the path. They paused and saw Tony fumbling with his camera.

"Tony, come on," Cal urged, going back and grabbing Tony's arm. Tony shook him off.

"I have to get my own pictures. No one will believe this unless I do," Tony breathed. He held up the camera and took a few photos of each creature. The flash momentarily blinded everyone in the clearing. Bigfoot roared and retreated into the cave. The dogman growled and started walking over to Tony, gaining speed as it crossed through the clearing. It veered off into the bushes alongside the trail and disappeared from sight.

Cal didn't like not being able to see the creature. A sneak attack that they couldn't see coming could be deadly. He reached into his pocket and pulled out the hunting knife that he always carried on hiking trips. "Now, damn it!" he shouted, pushing Tony in the direction of the path. Tony gave a glance at the video camera, then waved in its direction as he joined Cal and Aaron.

They were halfway down the trail when Cal looked around and saw that the dogman was following them. "Guys, we need to get out of here," he panted. Aaron turned around, as well, then picked up his pace to a near sprint. "I'll get the car ready," he shouted as he disappeared from sight.

Tony stopped running. His breathing was heavy. "I need a minute," he said.

"We don't have time," Cal insisted. Off to their right side, the bushes shook, and a low growling sound filled the air. The dogman stepped back out onto the trail, this time on four legs. It looked like an enormous wolf.

Tony couldn't believe it. This was what Talia had seen crossing the road, and he understood her confusion at thinking it was a normal, if unusually large, common animal. "Just one more picture," he said. He lifted the camera. The moment the dogman saw Tony's arms lifting, it charged at him.

Cal felt the hit, too. The impact dropped him to the ground, and his face hit a couple of rocks. Pain exploded in his head, and he felt blood running down his cheek. His arm jerked, and he realized that his knife had sliced his forearm before falling to the ground. He had no time to examine the cut before he regained his nerves and looked around for the weapon.

He grabbed the knife from the ground, rolled over, and saw that Tony was on his back. The dogman's front legs were on Tony's chest, with one of the paws close to Tony's neck. Its snout, long and powerful with sharp fangs hanging out of the mouth, snapped at Tony's face. Tony screamed.

The creature snapped at him again, then suddenly jumped away from Tony and whimpered. It was shaking, and huddled at the edge of the path, low noises coming from its chest and throat. Cal looked up and saw two men standing a few feet away. He recognized them as being the other cryptid hunters he had seen earlier. One of them held a taser in his hand and stared down at both it and the dogman in amazement.

"How did I get so close to it?" he asked in wonder. They all turned to focus on the dogman as it growled again, then bared its teeth and pounded the ground with its front paws. Sensing that it was overpowered, the monster retreated into the forest.

Tony groaned, and Cal got up from the ground with the help of one of the other men. "I'm Nate, and this is Mike," he said. "We saw you drive down here and thought you might need some help. Your friend is waiting in the parking lot with Stan Smith, the owner of this property."

"Oh, shit," Tony said as Mike helped him sit up. "I'm bleeding. So are you, Cal."

"An accident with my knife," Cal said. "And my face hit a rock." He picked up the knife and placed it back in his pocket. "Thankfully these guys had a taser and the presence of mind to use it." He looked at his friend's body. "He cut your leg. It looks pretty bad. Can you stand?"

Tony nodded. Cal and Mike helped him up, and the four men made their way to the parking lot. Stan was leaning against his truck, a shotgun in his hand. He was chatting with Aaron through the car window. "What happened?" Aaron asked as Cal and Tony reached the vehicle.

"It attacked," Cal said flatly. "The dogman. Let's get out of here and go the clinic."

"I expect that you won't come back," Stan said. "There's a reason I bought this land and placed all those warning signs around."

"Yes, sir," Tony said meekly. Cal was silent. The signs had not kept Tony away from the cave. The attack by the dogman had injured him, but it might have been the one thing that would make him stay away from this land as long as they were in Tahoma Valley. "At least I have proof," he said proudly as he sat in the car. "We'll look at the pictures later."

"What are we going to tell the doctor?" Cal asked when the doors were closed and Aaron had started the car.

Tony shrugged. "Animal attack. A dog running around. I'm sure it's nothing they haven't seen before."

Cal nodded. As they left the other men behind, he turned away and tried to relax. They were out of danger, and he hoped they'd never return to this place. He had already seen two monsters, and he didn't want to see them again. However, he knew their night wasn't over. They had already been planning to go to the clinic. They now had a valid reason to be there.

Mike, Nate, and Stan watched as Aaron backed up the car and drove quickly away from the lot. "What happened down there?" Stan asked.

"We saw a dogman attack Tony," Nate said. "We came with a taser, and I didn't even think. I just ran up and hit it, and was pretty effective at getting it to back away."

"I wonder why it's here," Mike said. "I've only ever heard of Bigfoot around Mount Rainier. Not any upright canines."

"It may not last long in these parts," Nate said. "I noticed that it had a wound on its back. I think it got into a fight with something bigger and stronger."

All three men heard the howling sound that eerily responded to their comment. "I think it's time to leave," Stan said. "It's been nice having you guys here, but I'm sure you'll want to rejoin your friends now."

Mike and Nate took the hint. "Yes, sir. Thanks for letting us come down here." Stan drove them back to his house, then watched as they drove away in their own cars. He locked his front door behind him and settled in for the night, trying to shake the feeling that he was being watched.

CHAPTER 11

"I'm so sorry," Talia said, and tears came into her eyes. She sat back down on the couch.

"You should go look at the cameras," Autumn told Zach. She sat on the arm of the couch and waited for Talia to calm down before repeating her question. "How long have you known Tony, and why did he send you here tonight?"

"I met him on Saturday night," Talia said. "And he didn't really send me here. He asked me to do him a favor, and I demanded payment for it. He accepted my terms. I figured if I was going to agree to come over here and tell you a story about Bigfoot, I might as well get something out of it."

Over at the table, Zach watched as the shape in the cave retreated into the darkness within. One of the men waved at the camera before trying to take a picture and running away from the clearing. Brown fur came into the picture, at the very bottom of the screen, and he quickly pressed the button to take a photo. "Show yourself," he muttered. To his surprise, he caught part of an ear, standing up from the top of the head, and took another photo. The ear disappeared and a large wolf emerged from somewhere behind the camera, walking across the clearing. It was quick, but Zach thought he pushed the right button in time to get at least part of the creature in focus. The video kept running for a bit, then stopped as it waited for something else to make a move within the range of its sensors.

He looked up and noticed Talia and Autumn watching him. He was very annoyed that the woman had wasted his time, and wanted the same answers that Autumn did. "He gave you money to tell me lies?'

Talia nodded, wiping her eyes. "Yes. I would normally never do this, just flat out tell stories to complete strangers. But something happened just before I met Tony that made me completely vulnerable to believing him."

She explained her reasons for coming to Tahoma Valley, and why she had been out on the road on Saturday night. "I did see something then. Not a Bigfoot, something else. I came across Tony and his friends, and was so relieved to be around other people that I told them about the big wolf I saw on the highway. Tony listened to what I had to say and told me I might have seen a dogman."

"Why should we believe this?" Autumn demanded with her arms crossed. "For all we know, you've known Tony for years."

"Ask him and his friends," Talia suggested. "They wanted me to come over here and distract you from going down to some cave that they were obsessed with. Well, not the cave itself. They're looking for Bigfoot. They also kept looking at drawings of a building in town."

"Did they tell you what building it was?" Zach asked, coming over to sit down across from Talia again. He studied her, still doubting everything she said.

She thought back to when she had been at the tavern with them. "It was the clinic. The medical clinic in town. They said they were meeting someone late at night because of a busy schedule during the day."

"Why would they need a map of the building?" Autumn asked.

Zach thought he knew why. He picked up his phone and dialed the number for the sheriff's office. "May I speak to Deputy Brown?" he asked when the phone was answered and he had introduced himself.

"Deputy Brown is currently out on patrol, sir," a firm male voice told him. "Deputy Singleton is almost off shift, but I can see if she'll speak to you."

"Thank you." He saw Autumn move away from the door and sit closer to Talia. They started whispering, and he could tell that Autumn was starting to believe whatever Talia was telling her.

"Hi, Zach, can I help you?" Joey's tone was curt, and he wondered what kind of night it had been in town.

"Hi, Joey. Listen, I think someone is going to try to break into the clinic tonight." He stood and moved away from the two women. "Into the vault, I mean," he added quietly.

Joey paused on the other end. "The vault?"

"Look, Reilly knows I know about it. There's some sort of secret room, isn't there? You might want to send someone over to make sure nothing happens to it tonight."

"Thanks, Zach," Joey said, now sounding slightly amused. "I'll take care of it myself. Have a good night." She hung up.

Zach rejoined the women. "So, Talia, is there any bit of truth to the story you told me on camera?"

She shook her head. "That was all Tony's idea." She pulled a folded piece of notebook paper out of her pocket and handed it to Zach. "This is what he wrote. I did see that other creature, though."

Autumn took the paper from Zach and read it out loud. After she was done, Zach reviewed the footage he had recorded, then gestured for Autumn to come over. As he deleted the interview, he came to a decision. "Can we trust her on this?"

"Something scared her enough to get her to talk to Tony, Aaron, and Cal," she said. "She said she approached them first, otherwise they probably never would have paid any attention to her."

He nodded. They both looked at Talia. "Are you willing to tell us the real story this time?" he asked. "And if there's enough to put on the show, are you willing to swear that it's true, and that it can appear on an episode of *Creature Hunt*?"

"Yes," Talia said firmly. "I hope Tony finds trouble with whatever he's out doing tonight. I'm not trusting him again."

"Good choice," Autumn said. She retreated behind Zach, and he set up the camera again. They restarted the interview, and as Talia's story progressed, Zach became more and more certain that there was real danger lurking in Tahoma Valley.

"I think you'll need some stitches. This is a fairly deep cut. How did you say it happened?" Carson Smith asked Tony. They were in an exam room at the clinic. Aaron was sitting across the room. Cal had declined to join them despite his wounds. Instead, he had asked for bandages and cleaned up in another exam room down the hall, with a nurse checking him out briefly before he went back out to the waiting room at the front of the clinic.

The cut on his arm was superficial. He had taken some extra gauze and tape in case he needed them, and had asked the nurse for some ibuprofen for the pain. He was still hurting, and knew he'd have some bruises, but he needed to be alert for the next part of the night's plans. He had Tony's backpack with him, which was empty for the moment.

Tony shrugged. "I guess someone's dog wandered away and got aggressive."

Carson looked at him sharply. "Are you sure? We don't see very many stray dogs around here."

"Why is that, Doctor Smith?" Aaron asked. "I thought people in rural places always kept dogs."

Carson struggled to keep his temper in check and looked for the supplies he needed. "Not around here. If people do have pets, they keep them in fenced yards or in the house." He collected his items and placed them on a tray, washed his hands, and put on gloves. "Would you like an anesthetic, Tony?"

Tony nodded. Aaron used the moment to text Cal and let him know that the doctor would be busy for the next several minutes. Cal sent a thumbs-up sign in response. Aaron sat back and kept his eyes on his phone as the doctor gave Tony a shot, cleaned the wound, and began to sew the skin on his leg back together.

Down the hall, Cal approached the front desk, manned by the nurse and a security guard. He asked to use the bathroom and both of them nodded. He slipped past all of the exam rooms, and finally found Dr. Smith's office. He entered the room and closed the door just enough to leave some light from the hallway. He tried the two doors that were on the opposite wall. One was a closet, and the door opened easily. The other door was locked.

"Not surprising," Cal whispered. He walked softly to the

desk and opened the top drawer. No keys. He looked in two drawers on the side. No keys.

"And what brings you in tonight?" he heard someone saying. He dropped down behind the desk.

"I was out hiking and slid off the trail," another voice replied. He chanced a look around the desk and saw the nurse walk by with two men. One of them was limping. "Really scraped it up."

"That's too bad," the nurse replied. "Let's see what we can do for you." He heard the door of the exam room next door close.

"Where are they?" Cal muttered. He saw a white lab coat hanging on the coat rack behind the door. It was tucked against the wall, and would be hidden by any other coat that was placed there. He snuck over and checked the pockets.

Two keys jingled, and he smiled. He pulled out a keyring and had to put his hand over his mouth to keep from laughing. It was in the shape of a walking Bigfoot. He took the keys over to the locked door and the first one he tried fit easily into the lock. Cal turned it and opened the door.

He was faced with a dark staircase. He looked around for a flashlight, but it was getting late and he didn't want to waste any more time. He quietly shut the door to the office and felt around for a light switch at the top of the staircase. He found it, and a singular bulb at the bottom of the stairs illuminated the way.

Cal walked quietly down the stairs, trying to be quick without falling down. At the bottom, a long hallway led to a second door, this one made of dark wood. He pulled out his cell phone and turned on the flashlight function, lending a better view of the neatly swept floor. He crept down the hall, curious about why this passage had been built.

He fit the second key into the heavier door, surprised at how easy this was turning out to be, and wondered how often the doctor was down here. Probably fairly often, he reflected. The locks weren't sticking or rusty, and the walls were clean and free of dust.

He opened the door and slid into an air-conditioned room. The faint light from the hall was enough to show him another light switch, and he turned it on. He stood still, stunned at what he saw.

Bookcases lined the walls, filled with photos and plastic bags. Cal's brief glances at them revealed clumps of hair and labels describing where they were found and the time frame. He ignored the photos on the walls. His eyes went straight to a counter where a torn backpack sat. It was green with a reflective stripe across the back, and several dark stains made him think that whoever the pack had belonged to was now probably dead.

It wasn't precisely what he had been told to collect, but Cal picked it up and folded it so it would fit in Tony's bag. As he did, a couple of broken glass vials fell out, and shattered on the floor.

"Damn," he said, looking around for a cloth. He saw a sink in the corner with some paper towels, and used them to clean up. He put the used towels in the outside pocket of the backpack. While placing the roll back on the counter, his eyes fell on the skin and hair sample that Tony and Aaron had described to him.

It was in a large plastic bag, and the blood inside looked to be dry. Tony had been very anxious to get this particular sample, as he had only received a small piece of it at the lab. Cal picked it up gingerly and placed it next to the backpack. He closed the bag, looking around to see if anything else could be useful.

His eyes fell on two bookcases enclosed with glass doors. Inside the first one, he saw what appeared to be a preserved Bigfoot hand. He was instantly tempted to grab it, but stopped himself. The backpack looked like it had been set aside and forgotten on the counter, perhaps not considered important to the doctor. But something of this size was sure to be missed, especially as it appeared to be the only such item in the room.

He stepped over to the other bookcase. Through the glass,

he saw several bones laid out on the shelves. Bells started ringing in his head, and he thought that Tony would appreciate being able to run tests on at least one of those bones. There were enough of them that one would most likely not be missed. He used a paper towel to open one of the doors and removed a small bone. There was no label on the bookcase, so he had no idea if these were supposed to be from Bigfoot.

He closed the door and backed away, then took several pictures with his phone. Tony would have to be satisfied with the pack and the sample, along with the bone. Cal wanted to get out of this room, because it was starting to feel creepy.

Cal made sure the door was locked behind him and hurried down the hall. He crept up the stairs and very quietly opened the door, grateful that the office was still dark and empty. He turned off the stairway light and locked the door, then returned the key.

Tony hadn't been specific about how Cal should get the evidence out of the clinic. He didn't want to walk openly out of the building with it, in case someone asked to check inside his bag. He looked outside into the darkness and noticed that the office was at the very back of the building. A lone light, hanging somewhere on the rear of the building, showed him patches of grass and dirt leading to a dark shed at the edge of the property. He opened the window, quietly dropped the bundle onto the ground, and breathed a sigh of relief.

He opened the door to the office and was nearly blinded by the hallway lights. He blinked, and a voice behind him made him jump. "Can I help you, sir?" the security guard demanded. He looked at Dr. Smith's office door and frowned, then reached around Cal and closed the door with a firm click of the latch.

"My friend is in an exam room," Cal explained. "Sorry, I guess I got lost after I used the bathroom."

"Your friend's name?" the guard snapped.

"Tony Simons," Cal replied. The guard nodded and gestured for Cal to follow him. He guided him to the door of the exam room and disappeared down the hallway.

Cal lingered in the doorway and saw that Tony's leg was now bandaged. "Hey, how much longer?" he asked casually. Aaron gave him a questioning glance, and he nodded.

"A few minutes," Dr. Smith said. "I just need to get a few pain pills together."

"Thanks," Tony said weakly. "Cal, maybe you should wait in the car."

"Sure," Cal agreed. He left the room and found his way back out to the reception area. A female sheriff's deputy was chatting with the receptionist. She studied him as he walked past the desk, and he tried to keep his face down and eyes away from her.

He got outside and shivered as he found his way around to the back of the clinic. The bag was still on the ground. He picked it up and heard a rustling sound in the bushes. "Not again," he whispered. He flicked on his cell phone light and held it out, searching the trees around him for any sign of an animal.

Two glowing red eyes blinked back at him. Not waiting to see anything else, Cal ran for the car and got there just as Tony and Aaron emerged from the clinic. "I got it," he told them. "Let's get the hell out of here. I'm done for tonight."

CHAPTER 12

The next morning, Autumn woke up late and went over to Cabin Two to eat breakfast with her friends. Zach had already gotten up and was reviewing the video footage from last night. Once she had gotten dressed and come downstairs, he had told her that he was going into town for a couple of hours.

After Talia had left last night, he had replayed the newly recorded footage, and was happy with her story. "It sounds a lot more authentic than the Bigfoot story," he had said to her. "And the wound on the back of the animal matches with the patch of skin that Mitzi found."

"Yeah, but what caused that wound?" Autumn asked. "Sounds like the dogman got into a fight with something. What animal do we know around here that would take on a creature like that?"

She ate nearly half of her cinnamon roll before really listening to what her friends were saying about the previous night. "We actually rescued Tony and his friends," Mike said. "There was a monster chasing them, a dogman. I don't know what I was thinking. I just ran up to it and used the taser."

"They were shaken up," Nate said. "I think they went to the clinic after that."

Autumn smiled. "Well, while you two were out almost getting yourselves killed, we had some intrigue of our own here."

"Yeah, what happened with that woman?" Erica asked. "By the time she left, I was already asleep and Bill didn't see anything except her car leaving the clearing."

"It turns out, she was being paid by Tony Simons to come over and distract Zach while he and his friends went down to the cave." She laughed. "I guess he didn't realize we'd have cameras up and would see him down there."

"What? What did she tell you?"

Autumn summarized Talia's original story about the

daytime Bigfoot sighting. "Once I saw Tony on the video and realized what was happening, we confronted her. She broke down and admitted that she had actually demanded payment in exchange for telling the story, because she wanted to get something out of it."

"People like that make actual sightings sound fake," Erica said in disgust.

"However, she then told us that she did see a monster. A large wolf crossing the highway at night, with a wound on its back, that then stood up on its hind legs and stared at her until she drove away."

"Whoa!" Nate exclaimed. "That sounds familiar."

Autumn nodded. "It was only because of that sighting that she spoke to Tony, Aaron, and Cal when she got back to her cabin. She's staying right next to them. Zach decided to believe her, and did end up getting her real interview on camera. She left with a vow to not have anything to do with Tony again."

"I would hope not," Erica said. She still looked angry. "But I do hope she kept the money. Serves Tony right for asking someone to do that."

"What do you suppose Tony's here for?" Nate asked. "What do you think they were hoping to find at the clinic?"

Autumn's friends knew that she believed there was a secret vault filled with proof of Bigfoot sightings. However, she decided to keep Zach's possible visit to that vault to herself. He didn't know for sure yet that he'd be going there tonight, but he was hopeful that he would finally see the evidence that had been collected from people over the years. If Zach was able to share anything, she would tell her friends about it. She didn't like keeping secrets, especially when they were all out in the field like this, but she rationalized that if the vault turned out to be nothing more than a few footprint casts and blurry photos, they wouldn't be missing out on anything.

"Let's hang out in town today," Erica suggested. "I'm sure there are plenty of things to see at the shopping center and the park."

"I'll agree to that if we can go out to the clearing behind the cabin tonight," Nate said. "Let's see what we can get on record for ourselves."

They all agreed to the plans, and cleaned up from their late breakfast. As Erica was telling Autumn about a gift shop window display the guys had seen the day before, Mike turned his attention to his laptop screen. "Hey, something happened over at the campground," he said, pushing back from the table. "A message just popped up on the sheriff's website."

Bill looked over his shoulder. "Disturbance reported at Rainier Lake Campground," he read. "Deputies on scene."

"Let's go," Nate said.

Autumn nodded. She was feeling restless and wanted to get away from the resort. "Okay. It's less than a mile from here."

Erica grabbed her car keys and they all piled in to her car. Mike rummaged through his backpack and checked his camera. "Full battery," he noted. "Good."

The group chatted about what they might find until Erica pulled through the campground gates. She passed the office and drove down one of the loops. Autumn kept her eyes peeled, but felt her phone vibrate as a text message came through.

Where are you? Zach wrote.

Exploring the area, Autumn wrote back.

She put her phone away as Erica turned on to another loop. "There!" Nate exclaimed. Several people were gathered outside the public bathroom. A nearby campsite looked to be in disarray, with trash thrown around the dirt and grass and a tent pulled out of the ground. Erica pulled over across from the site and they all got out of the car. Autumn saw Deputy Joey Singleton standing near the site, looking around. Mike was able to take a couple of pictures before she turned and frowned at the group.

"I think I can guess why you're here," she said as they

approached. "Please stay back."

"What happened, Deputy?" Bill asked. None of them, except for Autumn, felt comfortable enough to address Reilly or Joey by their first names.

"We're going to ask around about it, anyway," Erica pointed out. "We'd appreciate your perspective."

Autumn took out her phone again and held it high enough to get Deputy Singleton on screen. She pressed record just as the deputy gestured to the mess behind her. "A couple went hiking this morning. They had their trash in a bag on the cooler, intending to take it with them and leave it in the dumpsters by the restroom. They forgot." She pointed to a blue plastic cooler with its lid hanging on by one hinge. "When they returned about thirty minutes ago, they discovered this mess."

Autumn turned the phone to scan across the site. The cooler had been dented along with the damage to the lid. A trail of garbage, including napkins and food wrappers, led to the remains of a shredded black plastic bag. On a closer look, the tent had been knocked on its side, with sleeping bags and pillows tossed out onto the dirt and the stakes hanging in the air.

"Did anyone see this happen?" Nate asked, standing slightly behind Autumn.

Deputy Singleton shook her head. "No. As you can see, the closest sites are unoccupied. The couple staying here reported that there was a large hairy beast watching them from behind a tree when they got back. They called our office and ran to the bathroom for shelter when the monster hit a tree and yelled at them."

"Yelled?" Erica echoed.

The deputy shrugged and swept her long brown hair back behind her shoulders. "Their words."

"Here comes Reilly," Autumn said, turning off her video. She felt another text come in and looked up in surprise. A familiar figure was standing next to a picnic bench near the restrooms. It was Zach.

Come on over here.

She could see that he was talking to a couple, a man and a woman, who were sitting at the picnic table. Her eyes scanned the area, and she was amazed that she had missed his his truck. It was parked off to the side of the small gray brick building that housed the toilets and showers.

Be right there, she wrote back. She nudged Erica and showed her the text from Zach. Mike, Bill, and Nate had apparently already noticed him.

"Let me see what he's heard," she told them. "See if Reilly will talk to you, and look around if he'll let you." She walked over to the picnic bench, nodding to Reilly on the way as the deputy said something into his radio.

She reached Zach and squeezed his hand. "How did you end up here?" she asked quietly.

"I was leaving the resort and saw the deputies driving over here with their lights flashing. I followed, and found these two campers huddled in the men's room." He gestured to the couple at the table. "Devontae Morris and Tracy Brown, this is Autumn Hunter."

"Hi," Devontae said.

"It's nice to meet you," Autumn said.

"It was a damn Bigfoot!" Tracy exclaimed with tears in her eyes. "That deputy doesn't believe us, but it was."

"Not much scares me," Devontae admitted. "But that thing did. It was larger than any animal I've ever seen. It had grayish brown hair with a pointy head and an ape-like face. It had a horrible smell." He shuddered. "We would have noticed if it had been around the campsite earlier than today."

"You know what else was strange?" Tracy asked. "It appeared to only have one hand."

"You got a pretty good look at it?" Zach asked. He had been listening to them speculate about the creature for almost thirty minutes. Nothing they had said was new to him, but he appreciated that they had noticed the animal's missing hand and could give such a clear description.

"Yes," Tracy said, wiping her face with her sleeve. "He

saw us and raised both arms, then hit a tree with his hand."

"The whole tree shook and seemed to lean in one direction," Devontae said. "And then he roared. Or yelled. It made some sort of loud noise."

"We could only think to get over here," Tracy said. "Get some solid walls between us and that...thing."

Devontae put an arm around her. "When the police are done, we're leaving."

"Thank you for talking to me," Zach said.

"I saw food wrappers on the ground," Autumn said. "Was there any actual food in the bag?"

Tracy nodded. "We didn't eat all of the bacon and eggs we cooked this morning. It was stupid of us to forget the bag, but we had been planning to get in a hike around the lake."

Reilly rejoined the group. "Mister Morris, Miss Brown, we're done. If there's anything else you need to share, please call me." He gave his card to each of them. The couple slowly started walking back to the campsite. Autumn saw her friends helping to pick up the rest of the trash. Joey waited for Devontae and Tracy, then started to help them pack up their gear.

Another deputy appeared from behind the building. "There's nothing back there, Reilly."

"Thanks, Steve. You can head back to the office." Reilly faced Zach and Autumn, his face grim. "Joey is letting your friends look around the site as they help clean up. They already got some pictures of a couple of pretty clear tracks. Big tracks. Footprints."

"It's probably looking for food," Autumn said excitedly. "Something happened to the other Bigfoot, and now the surviving one has become more of a scavenger than a predator."

Reilly sighed. "This isn't the first time this has happened here this summer," he admitted. "In fact, this is the fifth such incident."

"Jessie told us about seeing a trashed RV on Saturday," Zach said.

Reilly nodded. "Seems like the creature is smelling food, and going for what's easy to come by."

"Mitzi said that there was a creature near her dumpsters," Autumn added. She saw Zach give a quick shake of his head, and changed her mind about sharing the rest of the story. "But I think that was probably something else."

Reilly appeared to not hear her as his radio came on. He responded. "Well, we're done here."

"What about our meeting tonight?" Zach asked.

Reilly sighed. "Carson agreed to eight o'clock. Be at the clinic on time."

"I will," Zach promised. Reilly joined Joey back at the site. They spoke briefly with Devontae and Tracy, then drove away. Zach and Autumn met up with their friends by Erica's car, trying to stay out of the way as the couple finished tossing their gear into their car.

Mike showed Zach the footprint photos. "Clear definition on these," he said.

Zach looked at them closely and agreed. "Send those to me," he said.

"So, what now?" Nate asked.

"Let's do what we were talking about earlier," Erica suggested. "Go into town and relax. We'll be out in the forest tonight, and I'd like to have some fun today. Lots of shops in town for all of us to look through."

"You mean, actually be on a vacation?" Bill asked with a quiet laugh. "Sounds good to me."

"I'm okay with that," Mike said. "There's nothing more we can do here anyway."

Zach was distracted by Devontae and Tracy. The couple kept looking over their shoulders at a visibly leaning tree. He couldn't get past the fear in their voices. This had been a genuine encounter, and he was worried that the Bigfoot was getting bolder. He hoped the couple would eventually be able to return to this area. He watched them drive away and waved to them, and was reassured when they waved back.

"What do you think, Zach?" Autumn asked, wrapping an

arm around him. Her touch brought his thoughts back to the present. He had the whole afternoon free before Carson and Reilly showed him the vault, and he didn't intend to spend all of it shopping.

"I'd like to stay out here a bit," he said. "I've never seen Rainier Lake."

Autumn studied him. She could tell that his mind was on looking for more evidence. Although he had been planning to not go out in the field himself, this was the perfect chance to look around. The nearest campers were back on the other loops, and Bigfoot had been seen here in the last couple of hours.

"I'll stay here with you," she offered. He nodded and smiled.

"Let's meet for an early dinner," he suggested to everyone. "How about the diner a little after five?"

They agreed, and Erica drove away with the three men arguing about which store they should go to first. Autumn had to laugh. As interested as her friends were in looking for monsters, they could also easily switch to something else without letting themselves be burdened by the evidence that was piling up in front of them.

Zach held Autumn's hand as they walked back to his truck. "A trail starts over there, near the restrooms," he pointed out. "Let's go for a walk and see what we can find."

Autumn's heart started beating faster. She hoped that they might find more tracks, some food left behind or dropped by the creature, or something even more compelling. Maybe they could get a clear photo, even multiple photos, of a Bigfoot.

"What are you doing here?" Talia asked. Tony, Aaron, and Cal had returned late last night, talking loudly when they got out of their car and sounding almost giddy. She had been awake, thinking about her encounter Zach and wondering why she decided to let Tony talk her into lying to him. She had fallen asleep vowing to avoid Tony until she left the resort tomorrow.

And now, here he was on the back porch of her cabin. She had come out here to enjoy the sounds of the creek and read a mystery book she had bought the day before. She had not had much time for reading in the last several months, and missed it. Tony had knocked on the front door, which she had ignored, and then she had heard him come around the side of the cabin until he finally reached her very comfortable and private spot.

"Hi, Talia. I just wanted to say thank you for distracting Zach last night." He was carrying a backpack that seemed to be filled with stuff.

She decided to not tell him that Zach and Autumn were on to him. "You're welcome. I'm not doing it again."

"Of course not. I gave you the money, right?"

"Yes."

"Okay." He paused, as if he wanted to tell her something else but wasn't sure what to say. "Did you sleep well?"

"Actually, yes," she said honestly. Once she had fallen asleep, she had not woken up again until the sunlight streaming through the windows finally reached her face. He took a few steps back, and she noticed that he was limping.

"Did something happen to you?" she asked, shocked at how much she hoped he had been injured.

"Just got cut by something. It will heal," he said. He shifted the weight of the backpack.

"Going for another hike?" she asked, pointing to the bag.

"Nope. Just need to carry this with me. Valuable stuff."

"Uh huh."

She was relieved to see his friends come around the side of the cabin. Aaron looked alright, but Cal had several bruises on his face, and his arm was covered in gauze. "Hi, guys. Rough night?"

"We survived," Cal said quickly. "Tony, we need to go over some things."

"Oh, yeah," he said, reaching his hand behind him and touching the bag.

They heard branches cracking on the other side of the creek. Tony jumped. "Is it coming here?" he asked wildly. Talia sat up, starting to get annoyed at Tony and his friends.

A large branch fell across the creek, and they saw a man in coveralls emerge from the forest. "Sorry!" he called out to them. "Just clearing some dead branches." Talia couldn't see what the patch on his uniform said, but she assumed he was a town or county employee.

"It's okay," she called. The man disappeared, and soon the branch was being dragged back through the other trees. They heard a truck start up and drive away.

"That doesn't mean it's not hiding somewhere nearby," Tony said. He looked across the creek again.

Aaron rolled his eyes. "Come on," he said quietly. He led Tony back around the side of the house. Cal remained behind, watching them until they disappeared.

"You didn't tell anyone about last night, did you?" he asked quietly. "Tony's a bit unwound today, as you can see."

"No crap." She decided that the less contact she sustained with this group, the better it would be for her. "No, I didn't talk to anyone except Zach and Autumn. I did speak to some of their friends, when I first got to their cabins." She was satisfied that as long as Zach and Autumn knew what Tony had done, that was enough. She didn't know the whole story about this history between the two groups, and had no desire to learn what had happened either at the cave or with their plans for the medical clinic.

"Thanks," he said. "Have a good day." He left, and she breathed a sigh of relief. She picked up the mystery novel again. Just underneath it was a newly acquired book about Bigfoot. She smiled at it, knowing it was next on her list to read. She slipped off her shoes, put up her feet, and settled down into her chair.

A few minutes later, she heard rustling on the other side of the creek. She stood and walked over to the edge of the water, dipping her toes in and shivering. "Hello?" she called out "Hello?" She got no response.

She turned to go back to her chair when she heard more rustling, and then a soft growl. She faced the other side of the creek again. She didn't think that Bigfoot would growl. That behavior sounded more like a wolf. A large wolf. Possibly a dogman.

She stood still and watched the foliage. She thought she saw the outline of a dog's face and the reflection of a couple of eyes looking at her. She gathered up her books and went inside, making sure the door was shut and locked behind her. She closed the curtains and made herself comfortable on the couch. She set her mystery novel aside and picked up the book on Bigfoot. She started reading and was soon lost in the story, becoming more and fascinated with legends of the creature.

CHAPTER 13

Zach opened the back of his truck. He was amazed that no one from any of the surrounding campsites had followed the sheriff's car over here to see if there was a problem. No one else was camping on this loop, but he could hear the shouts and playful screams of kids coming from just down the road.

Autumn looked around as he started rummaging through his bag. "Quiet right here," she noted, sharing his thoughts. "Good for us, I guess."

"Let's hope so," he said.

"I thought we weren't going to go out in person," Autumn said. Zach sighed and looked over at her. She had her arms crossed and a slight smile on her face.

"We know the cave is its home," Zach said. "I didn't want to go right back into its territory. Out here, the creature is probably looking for food or something else. Let's see if we can take advantage of that."

"Strike while the trail is fresh."

"Yes." He laid out the bear spray and a knife. "You can carry the bag. I'll have the camera, and take the lead as we walk."

"Okay," she agreed. He was used to doing a similar routine on the show, and it always seemed to work out for him and the crew. He could concentrate on whatever monster was suspected to be in the area, and his cameraman and security people could do their own jobs.

Zach placed what he needed in the bag and made sure the camera was charged. He then closed and locked the back of the truck, making sure the keys were easy to reach in the front pocket of his jeans. "Let's go find those footprints first," he said. Autumn placed the bag over her shoulders and followed Zach to the trail. It started at the back of the brick building and wound past Devontae and Tracy's campsite.

The footprints were fresh, and about an inch deep. Zach removed a tape measure from the bag and laid it down next to the print. "Eighteen inches," he noted, taking a few photos.

They moved on down the trail.

As they walked, Autumn scanned the forest around her. Squirrels climbed up and down trees, a deer appeared in the distance and started munching on some plants, and birds chirped. She didn't hear any branches breaking or see any movement that would make her think they were being tracked or followed.

It was half a mile to the lake. When they reached the water, they stopped to take in the view. Sun reflected off of the water, and in the distance several boaters were enjoying a day on the lake. A small beach had been carved out of this area of shoreline, and signs warned swimmers that entering the water was at their own risk. Buoy lines marked a small swimming area, and a floating dock was currently empty.

"I'm surprised there's no one here," Zach said, wiping sweat from his face with his sleeve. The day had warmed up to the high eighties.

"There's another larger swimming area closer to the campground entrance," Autumn said. "I saw the signs for it when we drove in. I doubt anyone finds this place unless they look at the trail map."

"Obviously either a park ranger or the sheriff's office put up those signs," Zach pointed out. Several ripples of water appeared just beyond the edge of the swimming area. "Some fish searching for food," Zach said.

"You hope," Autumn teased, and Zach blushed. He was squeamish about swimming in water where he couldn't see the bottom, and had never really enjoyed investigating lake or river monsters. She was sure there was something in his past that had caused such a reaction in him, but every time she had questioned him about it, he had refused to answer.

They followed the trail as it curved around the beach and entered the shelter of the forest again. Everything seemed to be normal until Zach stopped and Autumn almost ran into him. "Look," he whispered, pointing a trembling hand in the direction of the lake. The water could still be seen between the trees growing on the shore.

"What?" she whispered back, shading her eyes.

"Off the trail, over near the water's edge. Between those ferns."

Autumn's eyes followed Zach's finger to where the lake formed a small cove. A large stump by the water's edge made her hair stand on end. Her skin began to crawl as the stump reached a hairy hand into the water and brought it up to its face, taking a long drink.

"Oh my God." She was shocked that they had been able to get this close without Bigfoot noticing them.

Zach motioned for her to turn around. He slipped the bear spray out of the bag and forced it into her hand. He then checked his camera and made sure everything was in focus.

"Hey!" he shouted, startling Autumn. She was surprised that he would try to get Bigfoot's attention on them.

The stump slowly rose into the air. The familiar ape-like body shape and conical head appeared, and the creature turned its entire body around. It saw them and breathed out heavily, making a loud grunting noise. Autumn saw its head move up and down as it sniffed the air, and its eyes fell on her.

She stared at the creature. Two years ago, she had been trapped in a cave with it and her only thought had been to get hair and blood samples, then somehow get out of the cave alive. Time and experience now gave her an appreciation for why Zach had tried to keep both of them from direct contact with Bigfoot.

"I think it recognizes us," Zach said quietly. Bigfoot settled its eyes on him, and then raised both of its arms up in the air and roared.

Zach smoothly took several pictures. The creature roared again, then turned and walked away along the water's edge, making loud splashing noises and sending small waves out into the lake. The first few steps also sent tremors up the hill and rattled a few loose stones near Autumn. She clutched the bear spray, wondering just how much good it would have done if the creature had attacked them.

"Are you okay?" Zach asked, pulling her close to him.

"I think so," she said. "I just still can't get used to being so close to a creature that so many people refuse to believe exists."

"I don't think we're meant to get used to it." Zach looked at the photos. "Look at this," he said excitedly, showing Autumn the camera. Bigfoot's body was clearly visible. The colors were sharp, and the facial features were distinct. Caught mid-vocalization, its lips were pulled back in a grimace, and the dark eyes seemed to look straight at the camera.

"You'll use that on the show, and people will still say it's a fake," Autumn said. "Hey, let's get out of here."

Zach nodded. He wasn't anxious to keep following Bigfoot now. He had the creature on video, along with what could be part of the dogman. He had good pictures of the whole animal, and the footprint it had left behind at the campsite. He had interviews with people sharing their encounters with one or both cryptids. Depending on what he saw in the vault tonight, he thought there was more than enough footage to create a special episode of the show.

"Zach," Autumn urged, and he heard fear in her voice. He looked past her and realized that while they had been talking, another animal had discovered them.

The dogman sat in the middle of the trail, just beyond where they had seen the Bigfoot disappear along the shore. It wasn't blocking their way out, but Zach was sure that any attempt they made to run would lead to an attack. Still, he lifted the camera and took some pictures.

"It's just going to look like a wolf when it's sitting that way," Autumn protested quietly. "Just like the photos you got in Minnesota."

"Notice the quiet?" Zach asked. "That also happened with Bigfoot."

She had indeed noticed that once they had seen Bigfoot, the woods had seemed to shut down. It was a phenomenon that unnerved her. If regular forest animals were too scared to be around these creatures, maybe she and Zach shouldn't be here, either.

The dogman growled and moved its lips up into a sneer. There was a lot of intelligence behind the eerie yellow eyes, and Autumn wondered how such a creature could have come to exist. The dogmen she had encountered before had also emanated an evil feeling. She had never felt that in her Bigfoot encounters.

The creature rose to its back legs, coming to a height of roughly seven feet. Zach tried to get a picture, but felt his hands trembling. He, too, sensed the differences between this creature and Bigfoot. "Damn," he said.

Suddenly, a large, heavy shape emerged from the trees and a hairy arm swung out. Bigfoot's fist made contact with the dogman's snout, and the canine fell to the ground. It rolled over and stood up again, crouching down on its back legs to face Bigfoot. It turned its back to Autumn and Zach, and they saw the wound that Talia had described.

"I don't think this is their first encounter," Autumn realized.

"Maybe the dogman killed the other Bigfoot," Zach suggested. "The wounds Chase described sound like a dog attack."

"Do you know how crazy we sound?" Autumn hissed. "Let's get out of here."

The two creatures were still preoccupied with each other. The Bigfoot approached the dogman and the dogman started to back away in the forest, then lunged forward and nearly bit the Bigfoot's arm. Zach grabbed Autumn's hand. They hurriedly walked down the trail, the heat suddenly no longer a concern for them. When they reached the beach, they paused to take some deep breaths and make sure they weren't being followed.

"No monsters," Autumn breathed. She looked at all the boats still on the lake. Everything seemed back to normal. The animal sounds were back, and she saw birds flying over and settling on the floating dock. "Let's keep going."

They made it all the way back to Zach's truck, and didn't say anything else until the doors were locked and they had each nearly finished a bottle of water. "Please tell me you've never seen that before," Autumn said.

"When I was down in Oregon, in June, the Bigfoot and dogman seemed to have found a way to co-exist," Zach said. "I guess something happened around here that turned these two into enemies."

"Yeah, like the dogman killing a Bigfoot. I've had enough of cryptids for now," Autumn said. "I just want to take a shower and go join my friends for some fun."

Zach was concerned at the tone of her voice. He knew that she feared the dogman more than any other animal, cryptid or not. He put the truck in gear. "Let's get cleaned up back at the cabin and find a few stores that catch our interest in town," he suggested.

"Yes," Autumn said. She looked in the side mirror and was happy to see no sign of any animals as they left the campground.

"What was that?" Tony asked. It was late afternoon, and for the sixth time that day a thumping noise had come from behind their cabin.

Cal looked out the window again. "Nothing. Nothing's out there. I'm telling you, it's just a deer or something walking by."

Aaron sat on the floor, repeatedly looking at the hair and skin sample in the plastic bag. "This really doesn't look like the usual type of hair we get when people think they've seen Bigfoot. I'm guessing it might be from the dogman."

"It did have a wound on its back," Cal said. He had gotten a glimpse at it when it was on Tony, but had not paid much attention at the time.

"Talia's still over at her cabin," Tony said. He had been unfocused all day. "Maybe we should go say hi to her again."

"Let's leave her alone," Cal advised. "Look, we have what you wanted. Why don't we leave now and get this stuff out of Tahoma Valley before someone happens to notice that it's gone?"

"No," Tony insisted. "I bet that Autumn's group is going to be outside tonight. They always have a time when they use calls and wood knocks to try to get a reaction. If they do that, let's see if we can have a chat with them."

Cal sat down at the table and looked at the bloody backpack. "What do you think happened with this bag? I assumed the person it belonged to is dead."

"I doubt it," Tony said. "For some reason that bag looks familiar to me, but I don't know why."

A howl broke the otherwise peaceful sounds around the cabin. "Think that's a deer?" Tony snapped at Cal, looking out the window.

"No. But I also don't think it's the dogman, coming back for another round with you."

"Thank goodness Nate and Mike showed up last night," Aaron said. "That taser was useful. Maybe we should get one the next time we go out in the field."

Tony sat down at the table and finally stared at the last item Cal had removed from the secret room. It was the piece that had kept him on edge all day. He still couldn't believe that he was possibly holding a bone from a Bigfoot. If he could extract DNA from it, he could be the person that finally proved the existence of a new animal. It could be classified and protected, and it would all be due to his knowledge and efforts.

Cal seemed to read Tony's thoughts. "Hey, don't get ahead of yourself. The cabinet wasn't labeled like the others. We don't know what that bone belongs to."

"You heard Bill shouting about a dead Bigfoot at the tavern the other night," Tony argued. "There's only one conclusion to draw from that."

"Cal's right," Aaron said, joining them at the table and running his finger along the edge of the bone. "Let's wait to do some testing. It'll take time, Tony. You know that."

Tony sat back and nodded. He knew his friends were just

trying to calm him down, but they were right. Cal's additions to Tony's request, the backpack and the bone, were intriguing, but his questions weren't going to be answered in just a couple of days.

Another thump came from the forest. This time, it did sound like something was hitting a piece of wood against a tree. Aaron frowned. "The BOG group wouldn't be out this early, would they?"

Tony shook his head. "Let's think about what to get for dinner. Later on, we'll go over to their cabin and see what they're up to. Make sure everything goes back in my bag. I don't want to leave anything behind here that might attract Bigfoot."

CHAPTER 14

After having dinner with Autumn and her friends at the diner on the edge of the shopping center, Zach said goodbye to Autumn and watched as she and the others drove away. They were heading back to the cabin, and should be getting settled in soon for their evening investigation. He was certain they would get responses to either the recordings or the tree knocking.

He wandered past the gift shop and studied the window display again. He saw the sweatshirts and decided it would be fun to have one. The image of Bigfoot was a familiar picture, and the words "Tahoma Valley" were printed across the front of the shirt. He went in and picked one out, then decided to get a keychain for Autumn.

He approached the counter and looked around for a sales person. "Hello?" he called out.

Zach saw Chase Brown emerge from the stock room in the back. "Hi, Chase," he said. "How are you?"

"Doing well'" Chase replied. "I see you found this shop."

Zach nodded. It was a mix of Tahoma Valley souvenirs and Bigfoot-related items. There was also a variety of locally crafted hand soaps and lotions, along with guide books for the mountain. "Do you own this store?"

"Yep. Opened about five years ago." Chase rang up the items and Zach paid. "Have you been finding anything interesting out there?" He gestured in the general direction of the forest beyond the strip mall.

"Yes." Zach studied Chase. "Do you have a few minutes? If you're willing, I'd like to interview you for the show."

"About finding the Bigfoot body?"

"Yes. And the ape suit."

Chase's face flushed. "I guess Reilly told you about that. It was stupid."

"Yes, it was." Zach shared a story about a similar incident at an Oregon winery in June, one where the man wearing the ape suit had been assaulted by something bigger than him.

"It's good for viewers to realize that sometimes what they think they are seeing really is just a hoax."

Chase checked the time and headed to the front door. "Did you find anyone else who saw the body?"

"George Smith."

Chase nodded. "I guess that's not surprising. It was on his father's land."

He let Zach out to retrieve his camera, then locked the door. They set up an area at the back of the store with a couple of chairs. On the wall was a neatly painted mural of Mount Rainer, and Zach thought it was a good backdrop for the scene. Chase sat down, Zach set up his equipment, and soon the two men were engaged in a discussion about pranks and hoaxes.

After asking Chase about finding about the body, and hearing the gruesome description of the injuries again, Zach looked at his watch. It was a quarter to eight, and he needed to go over to the clinic. "Thank you," he said as he collected his camera and gear. "I will contact you if I use any of it in the show."

"It's a relief to not have that secret anymore," Chase admitted. "Good luck with the rest of your trip here."

"Thanks."

Zach rushed back to his truck, and drove over to the clinic. Reilly was leaning against his car, obviously waiting for him. Zach parked the truck and took only his phone with him. He thought the two other men would probably object to any video recording of the items he was about to see.

"Hey, Zach," Reilly said. "You sure you want to do this?"

"Yes. I left a message for Joey last night, saying that Tony Simons and his friends were probably going to try to break in to the vault."

Reilly nodded as he opened the clinic door for Zach. He waited until they were down the hall and just outside Carson's office before responding. "She came over to check on them. They were all within sight of a clinic employee the entire time they were here."

"Are you sure?"

Reilly shrugged. "One of them got lost finding the bathroom and the security guard eventually found him."

Zach's stomach twisted. He had a feeling that somehow Tony, or more likely one of his friends, had managed to sneak something out of the secret room. Carson opened the door to his office and invited them inside. "Have you been down there to check to see if something is missing?"

"No," Reilly said patiently. He turned to Carson. "Zach is worried that one of Tony's friends got down there last night."

"I doubt it," Carson said. "But let's see, shall we?"

He held up a couple of keys and opened a door that was closely set into the wall. "Where do you keep the keys?" Zach asked.

"That's my secret," Carson said. "Now, before we go down here, let's go over a few things. No videos. You can only take pictures of individual items, not the whole room. I'm sure I can't stop you from confirming the existence of this room to a few select people."

"That's correct. I'm not going to keep it from Autumn."

"If you mention it to anyone else, I'd suggest you refer to it as 'a Bigfoot enthusiast's collection' and don't go into detail about anything else. Does all that seem fair?"

Zach considered it. "Yes. In return, if I want to use any pictures that I take down here, I will consult you first and get your approval."

Carson looked at Reilly, and the deputy nodded. Carson turned on the light at the top of the stairs and the men walked down. A long hallway, reminding Zach of the halls in the clinic upstairs, led to a second door. "What was this room originally used for?" he asked.

"It's always been for storage of important items," Carson said. "It was built at the same time as the clinic, but when we added on to the main building most of the medical items were moved into closets up there, so they could be accessed more easily. Now, it's just for stuff that relates to Bigfoot."

He opened the door, and motioned for Zach to walk in.

Zach noticed the cool temperature of the room and how silent it was. There was a long counter with a sink in the corner, and a couple of reddish stains on the floor. Reilly closed the door behind him and stood against it. Carson didn't even look over in the direction of the counter, but instead stood beside Zach.

"How have you kept all of this a secret?" Zach asked, his eyes roaming around the room.

"Through trust and dedication," Carson said.

"And a lot of luck and smooth talking," Reilly added.

Zach headed straight for a bookcase with glass doors. There, perfectly preserved, was a giant hand that ended in an abrupt cut. He snapped a picture of it, then turned to Carson to ask the obvious question. "Is this from the creature I injured?"

"Yes." Carson moved to the center of the room. His arms were crossed, and kept his eyes on Zach.

Reilly shifted into a more relaxed pose, leaning against the wall next to the door. "As you can see, this vault was handed down to us. Over in that corner you'll find some hair and print casts collected forty years ago."

"And pictures from before that," Carson added.

Zach eagerly headed to the shelves Reilly had pointed to. There were five specimen jars, each carefully labeled as "Hair—Reported to be Sasquatch." He took pictures of the bottles and three of the four plaster casts. There was a cast that looked odd to him, so he skipped past it and moved on through time.

Blurry photographs had been placed in plastic sleeves and tacked up to one of the room's walls. He saw dates spanning the past seventy years, and studied them. A lot of the photos were perfect examples of similar ones he had seen countless times before: an out-of-focus, large furry animal, crouching behind a bush or standing next to a tree, or a hulking figure walking through a field.

Zach understood the lack of clear photographic evidence. People could be shocked at seeing something so unusual, and by the time they reached their cameras and were able to get a picture, they were often shaking from nervousness, or the animal had moved on. That was one of the reasons he had added a video camera near the cave. Strapped to the tree, it would remain steady and hopefully catch clearer footage.

The camera had certainly caught some images last night, he reflected. He was still angry with Tony and his friends for heading out into the dangerous area, yet glad that they had drawn both the Bigfoot and the dogman into sight. The photos and videos he had been able to get were valuable evidence, and he was looking forward to using it on the show.

He lingered over a few of the recent photos. One was labeled as having been taken just this past January at Mitzi's Cabin Resort. "Is Mitzi's resort open all winter?" he asked as he took a photo of the picture. It showed a supposed Bigfoot across the creek from the resort, dragging a large tree limb.

"Yes," Reilly said. "The roads around here are open all year, so guests stay at Mitzi's when they come for skiing up on the mountain."

Zach turned and headed to the bookcases lining the opposite wall. One was empty, and the others were sparsely populated with jars and other objects. He found more hair samples, a preserved chunk of skin, a few bones, and more plaster prints. One of the prints, he noted, was thinner than the others and had four distinct claw marks at the end. He took more pictures.

"Was this supposed to be a Bigfoot print?" he asked casually, pointing to the plaster cast that had been placed on its own shelf.

"That was the suggestion," Carson. "You see how it's different, right?"

"Yes. It looks like tracks I've seen in other places."

"What would you say it is?" Reilly asked.

"Based on what I've heard and seen on this trip, I think it belongs to something called a dogman."

"Dogman?" Carson repeated. Zach saw a change in

Reilly's demeanor. Carson saw it, too. "Do you know about this, Reilly?"

"I've heard stories," the deputy said quietly. "That cast was made twenty years ago, though. I figured it was merely a legend, or had disappeared or died."

"I think there's one here now, and it's disturbing the Bigfoot in the cave. That may be why there were so many sightings recently, because the Bigfoot has been trying to get the dogman to leave."

"But sightings starting declining before you arrived," Carson pointed out.

Zach shrugged. "People went back to their regular lives after a day or two of walking through the forest with their cameras. For most people, the idea of finding Bigfoot sounds a lot better when you're at home in a comfortable chair than when you're out in the woods and realize that the chance of seeing one is incredibly slim."

"Then there are people like your girlfriend," Carson said. "She doesn't give up."

"No," Zach said. "She's very serious about proving that Bigfoot exists."

"And you?" Carson asked.

Zach wandered over to the hand in the display case. "I'd like to let people know that Bigfoot is more than a legend."

He looked around at the remaining pieces in the vault. He was relieved to have seen everything, but also disappointed that it was all being kept a secret. He examined the hand more closely, then turned to Carson. "Did you scrape some skin from this?"

"Yes," Carson admitted. "Every biological sample we get is sent to a lab."

"Where are the results?"

Carson shook his head. "They all come back as being inconclusive, or suspected to be tainted. Sometimes I wonder if the lab knows what's being tested and has its own agenda."

"So many layers of conspiracy," Zach muttered. "At some point, there will be a test that can exclude everything else and finally let science declare that Bigfoot is a species to be classed and studied."

"What about the dogman?" Reilly asked, the last word almost a whisper. He seemed afraid of saying the creature's name out loud.

Zach's gaze lingered on another bookcase. Through the glass barrier, he saw several bones sitting on the shelves inside. "When did you get these?" he asked excitedly.

"Back in June," Carson said. "Reilly received a report, from his cousin Chase, about finding a dead Bigfoot down by the cave. Reilly was busy for a few days, and by the time he got out there all he found in the area Chase described were those bones." Carson moved over to look at them. "We haven't sent them for testing yet." He frowned and appeared to be counting. "Reilly! One of the bones is missing."

"Are you sure?" Reilly asked.

"Yes. I was just down here on Sunday, looking around." He turned and scanned the room, his eyes falling on the counter near the entrance. "The backpack and the hair sample from Mitzi. They're gone, too!"

"So, someone did make it down here," Zach whispered. Carson covered his face with his hands and shook his head. Reilly walked over to the counter and studied the floor.

"Someone tried to clean up glass and blood," he said. "Probably spilled from the backpack."

"Autumn's backpack?" Zach asked. "You kept it down here?"

"Yes. Obviously, we should have kept it better protected. And I hadn't gotten around to locking up the sample yet." Carson shook his head. "We have to find those things."

"I think you just need to talk to Tony," Zach said calmly. He took a few pictures of the bones, oblivious to the panic that Carson and Reilly seemed to be feeling. "Was the hair and skin sample tested yet?"

"We sent a piece to the usual lab. They returned it, which is why I was down here on Sunday," Carson said. "There was no response about what species it came from."

Zach had a suspicion that Tony Simons worked for the lab that had received the sample. He might have tested it and realized that he could get better results by getting the whole piece of skin to prove that a monster was roaming the forest near Tahoma Valley. "Were you thinking it was from Bigfoot?"

"We weren't sure. That's why it went to the lab," Reilly said. His cell phone rang, and he moved to the other side of the room.

"Where do you think it was from?" Carson asked.

"I think it was from the dogman. The creature we've been seeing around has a large wound on its back."

"Hey, Zach, that was one of Autumn's friends," Reilly said, ending the call. "He said they're under attack from both Bigfoot and the dogman." His voice sounded strained.

"Let's go," Zach said, his emotions taking over. He had seen what he wanted to see. Autumn needed him now.

The three men left the vault, both Carson and Reilly making sure the door was locked. They hurried along the hall and emerged through the door in Carson's office. Zach ran out of the clinic and started his truck, hoping to get back to the resort before something terrible happened to Autumn.

CHAPTER 15

Autumn stared at the photos that had just come in from one of the trail cameras. From its position, it looked like it was the one Zach had left where the highway met the road to Stan's house. There were several blurry images of a large hand grabbing at the camera, and then one up-close image of the iconic large feet of the creature. Nate sat down and tried to do some measurements. "I think about eighteen inches," he finally said.

"The same as the prints we saw at the campground," Autumn said. "It knows we're looking for it."

"What do you think happened to the little one?" Erica asked, her voice filled with emotion. She had a soft heart for young animals, even those that stole people's backpacks and, according to science, didn't even exist.

"It probably set out on its own," Autumn said. "That's why the remaining Bigfoot is rummaging in dumpsters. It probably has had difficulty hunting, even with one remaining hand, and has learned that humans can be a source of food."

"I just hope it sticks to dumpsters," Mike said. "Okay, let's go."

"We'll be right behind you," Erica said, and the men went ahead to the clearing to set up their equipment.

"What do you think Tony's up to tonight?" she asked as she and Autumn filled a thermos with coffee and packed cups in a tote bag.

"Don't know, don't care. For some reason, he seems to think that Zach and I are competing with him for fame as cryptid researchers." She sighed. "Tell me, am I really that obsessed?"

Erica laughed. "You want the truth?"

Autumn rolled her eyes. "Come on. I wouldn't send someone to another researcher to tell a fake story just on the chance that I'd be distracting them from doing field research themselves."

"True. Ready?"

"Yep."

"I still can't believe you saw the Bigfoot again," Erica said to Autumn as they walked over to the clearing. It was a little less than a quarter mile from the cabin, and far enough into the forest that they were unlikely to be noticed or disturbed. The last time they had come out here, they had been interrupted by locals wanting them to leave. Autumn hoped that wouldn't be repeated tonight.

Autumn nodded and shifted the weight of the two camping chairs she was carrying. "No doubt it was the same creature. Zach got a good picture of its arms up in the air. I was able to see him as he usually is on the show, calm and confident in the heat of the moment." She smiled. "Kind of sexy, actually."

Erica rolled her eyes as they entered the clearing. The men had already set up a small table with a laptop and a separate audio recorder. "What should we start with tonight?" Bill asked. Autumn and Erica opened their chairs and settled into them. "I have a few vocalizations to try."

"Yeah, let's open with that," Nate suggested. They all got comfortable and let a deep silence descend on the clearing. Autumn shivered and zipped up her hoodie, already wishing she had brought a blanket with her.

Mike pressed a button on the keyboard. A mournful, whooping cry filled the air. It was supposedly from a Bigfoot, recorded many years ago. Autumn wondered how many other people had used this call the same way her group was using it right now.

They waited but heard nothing. "Again," Nate urged. Mike nodded and played it one more time.

This time there was a response. A loud roar made Erica almost fall out of her chair. The two long whoops that immediately followed it brought Bill and Nate over to the computer. "Did you get that?" Bill asked quietly. Mike listened to the sound on his headset and nodded, eyes wide.

They waited, but heard nothing more, not even the usual rustling of small animals or insects chirping. Autumn felt the hair on the back of her neck standing up, and her feelings of dread returned. She tried to stay focused on what her friends were doing. It was difficult, and the sensation of being stalked overwhelmed her. "Something's out there," Erica said, looking over at one of the heavy flashlights sitting on the table. Autumn nodded.

"Let's try a few wood knocks," she suggested. Mike nodded and sat back, taking a drink of the coffee they had brought with them.

Autumn and Bill looked around the edge of the clearing for sticks or limbs large enough to make a clear sound against a tree trunk. They found a couple of heavy sticks in a pile of fallen tree limbs and walked to different sides of the clearing. Bill held up his stick. "First try," he said, and swung the stick at a large tree. It hit the trunk, emitting a solid cracking sound into the air that echoed through the woods around them. He followed that up with two more knocks and stumbled backwards from the exertion.

Nate ran over to keep him steady as they waited. After a couple of minutes, in which the whole team stayed entirely still, three return knocks sounded in the distance. "That sounded like it was coming from near our cabin," Erica said, turning to face that direction.

"I'll try," Autumn offered. She used both hands to swing her stick. The resulting noise made her jump, but she managed to hit the tree three more times. She dropped the heavy stick, her arms vibrating from the force she had used.

The response was immediate, but Autumn's heart dropped when she saw where it was coming from. At the edge of the clearing stood Tony, Aaron, and Cal. Tony held up a large stick and hit a nearby tree once more.

"What the hell are you doing here?" Autumn demanded. Anger rose up inside of her. "After that crap you pulled last night, you're lucky that you're even still alive."

"Yeah, why are you here?" Nate demanded. He edged closer to the table, where Mike had set out the taser.

Cal saw his movement and stepped forward, keeping a

hand over his windbreaker pocket. "Calm down. We heard noises and got curious."

"All the way over at your cabin?" Erica asked.

"Actually, we've been hearing stuff all day," Tony said. "Strange thumps from out in the forest. A couple of howls. Some wood knocks. Some growling noises that reminded us of the dogman. When we heard that Bigfoot recording, we decided to come take a look."

"You can leave now," Autumn snapped. "We're busy here with real stuff. Not listening to made-up stories delivered by someone being paid to distract us."

"Hey, you stayed put and weren't down at the cave, right?" Aaron said. "I'd say it worked."

"We had the cameras up. We weren't going down there anyway," Autumn told him.

Tony was about to reply when a large rock sailed across the clearing and landed right next to Aaron. He jumped, knocking into Cal. "Shit," he breathed. "Where did that come from?"

"Only one thing out here could throw a rock that size," Mike said, his voice trembling. "And it's over there."

They stood still, only moving their heads to look in the direction of a familiar roar, ending with another ominous whoop. Autumn felt chills run down her spine. Out of the corner of her eye, she saw Cal and Aaron turn to run back down the trail. Nate joined them, shouting that he would call for help.

Tony was shaking. "No," he said. "Not again."

The Bigfoot stepped out into the clearing. The creature stood still, turning its head slowly as if it was studying each of them for weaknesses. Erica started backing towards the table, but Mike was closer and read her mind. He picked up the taser and powered it on. Erica picked up one of the flashlights. She could easily use it as a weapon, even if it only bought her some time to run away. Bill looked around in panic, then a determined look came over his face and he bent down to pick up the stick he had used for the wood knocks.

Autumn's brain finally forced her to realize that the creature was hunting for something. She felt Erica forcing another flashlight into her hand and her fist closed around it with reassurance. She heard breathing behind her and stopped moving again.

Erica stepped back from Autumn. "Is that...a wolf?" she asked, her voice nearly hysterical. "On two legs?"

Autumn spun around. The dogman was a few feet behind her, its mouth curled up in a snarl that almost looked like a grin. She focused on its glowing yellow eyes and large fangs that couldn't quite fit completely in its mouth. It growled, then tipped its head to the side and sniffed. Its gaze landed right on Tony.

"Go away!" he yelled at it. It was then that Autumn noticed Tony was wearing a backpack that seemed to be rather heavy. It was slung over one shoulder and swinging around as he turned to look at both monsters. She saw that it was partially unzipped. A flash of green with a reflective stripe inside caught her attention.

"Is that my backpack?" she screamed at him. "I lost that two years ago. How did you get it?" It was covered in blood, and she was horrified to see some bloody paper towels sticking out of one the outer pockets. Tony couldn't have made it any easier for Bigfoot to track him down.

The Bigfoot's eyes landed on Tony, which meant both monsters were watching him. The Bigfoot picked up another large rock. The power of just its one good arm was evident to everyone as the rock sailed across the clearing and hit him on the side. He screamed and stumbled around, hitting his head on a tree and falling to the ground.

"Let's get out of here," Aaron told Cal. He picked up the backpack and both men ran back down the path. Bigfoot saw them leave and disappeared into the trees. Everyone heard large thumps and tree limbs breaking as the creature tore a path around the clearing in the direction of the cabins. Autumn's attention was drawn back to the dogman when she heard it growl again. It dropped to four legs and ran across the clearing, following Aaron and Cal down the path.

"Let's get out of here," Mike shouted. He grabbed the laptop and the recorder, dropped them in his backpack, and they all ran past Tony's body. Autumn thought she heard him groan, but didn't stop to check on him. She couldn't believe they were actually chasing after two monsters, but instincts led her to keep running until they saw the two cabins. The men kept going around to the front, but the dogman stopped running. It stood on its hind legs and she could see it looking in the direction of the creek and the clearing on the opposite side.

Autumn saw the dogman stop and dragged Erica off the trail with her. They ran around the building, seeking a place to hide. Autumn found one and pointed to it. Erica followed her, and they collapsed down beside the woodpile behind their cabin.

CHAPTER 16

"What is that?" Erica hissed tearfully. "Is that what Nate and Mike saw last night?"

"It's a dogman," Autumn whispered quickly. "I told you about it before."

"Yeah, but it's freaking terrifying in person."

Autumn agreed. She had not forgotten the aggressive nature of the dogmen she had encountered in Minnesota. Now that she was once again in the vicinity of one, she started to feel herself shaking. "What brought it here?" she whispered.

They heard a car pull up in front. Doors opened, and she recognized Reilly's voice. "Oh God!" Three shots rang out, and a vicious howl filled the air.

"I hit it!" Reilly shouted. "Damn, it's moving again!"

"Autumn?" Zach shouted. Autumn shook her head. She wasn't going to answer until she knew where either of the monsters were.

Another shot rang out, and another howl sounded. It was closer this time, and bushes along the side of the cabin started shaking. Erica grasped her flashlight, tears running down her face. Autumn grabbed her friend's arm and prepared to fight.

The dogman stumbled past them, walking on two legs, visibly wounded. It stopped and sniffed, then turned and saw the two women. Its eyes gleamed brighter with interest, and it tried to lunge at them before suddenly losing strength. A chilling moan came from its mouth. It turned away and disappeared into the forest. Autumn felt Erica's shaking arm lower, and the flashlight dropped to the ground.

Footsteps approached the back of the cabin. "Autumn?" Zach called out, filling both women with relief. "Erica?"

"Here!" Autumn replied, poking her head around the side of the cabin. Zach ran over to her. She was relieved to see that Reilly and Carson were with him. "I'm not sure where everyone else is."

"What's going on?" Reilly demanded. "I shot that wolf

thing. I think it ran away." His hand was on his gun, and he was looking around nervously. A heavy breeze came past the cabin, and the resulting waving of the foliage made him tense up. Autumn saw him put his hand on his gun.

"We better get inside," Erica said, but before they could move in that direction, they heard shouts from the clearing beyond the cabin.

Autumn grabbed Zach's hand, and he held on to her as the group moved back around to the front of the cabin. Mike, Bill, and Nate were watching as Aaron and Cal ran over to the creek, trying to escape from Bigfoot. The creature was stalking them along the edge of the forest, visible to everyone standing by Cabin Two.

Autumn saw the reflective stripe again and her emotions overcame her. "He has my backpack!" she shouted before releasing Zach's hand and starting to follow Bigfoot.

"The backpack from the vault?" Carson asked quietly. Reilly nodded in confirmation. Zach panicked, because he knew how Autumn had risked her life in order to retrieve the backpack before. He didn't want that to happen again.

As Zach, Carson, and Reilly set out to follow Autumn, Erica dropped to the porch. "I'm staying here."

"I'll stay with you," Bill agreed, putting an arm around her. "Let's make sure the dogman doesn't come back and surprise them." They kept the flashlights nearby and settled onto the porch.

"Let's go check on Tony," Mike told Nate. "The dogman was headed in his direction." Nate picked up his taser and agreed. The two men set out down the path. Erica called Mitzi to let her know what was going on, and told her they might need some assistance in getting someone out of the forest.

Mike and Nate reached the clearing just in time to see the dogman sniffing at Tony. "Here I go again," Nate said. He charged the taser, and nodded at Mike. Both men charged into the clearing and Nate hit the dogman with the taser. The first place he hit was near the neck, but the dogman shook off the attack with a smooth, sharp motion of its head.

Nate felt his hand slipping across the creature's bloody hide. He pulled away when feeling the scar tissue on its back sent a sense of revulsion through his body. The dogman saw its chance and put both front paws on Tony's chest.

Nate brought the taser up to the wound and jammed it down. The hide was thick, but the charge still did its job. Nate could feel the immediate pulse of electricity through the creature's abdomen.

The dogman jumped back and howled. It was still walking on two legs as it limped into the forest and turned its head to glare at them. Nate stood in front of Tony as Mike checked to make sure the other man was still alive. "He's breathing!" Mike exclaimed. The dogman slipped away into the forest, making the same throat and chest sounds it had the last time they had used the taser. Nate looked down at his clothing and realized that he had dogman blood all over him. "Let's get him back out to the clearing," he said.

He and Mike were just about to try to drag Tony down the path when Marvin and Mitzi showed up with a golf cart. Marvin helped them get Tony upright and into the back seat. Tony's eyes had opened and he was muttering something about Bigfoot, so they drove him back to Cabin Two and placed him in a chair on the porch.

"I need to get out of this," Nate said, and rushed into the cabin to change his shirt. He returned to the porch and hung the blood-stained shirt over the railing. Marvin and Mitzi tended to Tony's superficial wounds, feeling assured that Carson would look at the other injuries soon. Then, everyone waited for the rest of the group to return from the other side of the creek.

Cal and Aaron reached the clearing on the other side of the creek and turned around. They could see the outline of Bigfoot on the other side of the water. It had stopped just beyond the reach of the lights from the back of Cabin One, but Aaron knew it was still there.

"I told Tony not to bring that blood-covered backpack," Cal hissed. "Why did you pick it up?"

"You thought it was human blood, remember?" Aaron reminded him. "It looked like someone had been attacked and died, and the creature took the bag with it."

"I'm guessing the blood came from the broken vials that I saw," Cal said. "And that it's Bigfoot blood."

The monster let out a loud roar. One powerful jump allowed it to cross the creek and land in the clearing. It was now only twenty feet away from both men.

"We're going to die," Aaron whispered.

"No," Cal said. He took out the gun from his jacket pocket. "We're not going to die. That fucking monster is going to die."

"Don't do that," a voice called from the other side of the creek. Reilly Brown held his own gun at his side. "Don't shoot!" Autumn thought that was it was a strange order, given that the deputy had shot the dogman.

"If it comes any closer, I'll do it," Cal threatened. The sharpness of his voice chilled Autumn, and she jumped onto the nearest rock to cross to the clearing.

Zach followed her. He had armed himself with the bear spray, keeping his knife in his pocket. He moved beside Cal. "Let's try to keep it alive, okay?"

Aaron set the backpack on the ground. The Bigfoot watched his every move. "I think it wants what I have in here."

"My pack," Autumn said, grabbing the bag from him and moving away. When she tried to open the backpack, a bone and a plastic bag fell to the ground and they all looked away from the creature for a moment.

"A bone from the dead Bigfoot," Carson breathed. "Put it back in the bag."

Autumn looked at her bloody and crumpled backpack. "This had all sorts of evidence inside."

"It's all gone," Carson called out. He and Reilly seemed reluctant to cross over to the clearing. "It's of no use to us by now, anyway."

Bigfoot took a couple of steps in Autumn's direction, and the creature suddenly had their attention again. She looked at Bigfoot and was overwhelmed by the smell surrounding the creature. She noticed its missing hand and recalled the terrible sounds it had made when Zach had cut off the hand. Trembling, she finished opening Tony's bag and removed her torn and bloody backpack.

She dropped Tony's backpack to the ground, and Cal, seeing Reilly staring at him, replaced the bone and the skin sample. Aaron grabbed it and held onto it, knowing what it had meant to Tony to be able to prove that Bigfoot could be a classified and documented species.

Autumn walked closer to Bigfoot with her own backpack. Its full attention was on her. She kept an eye on its one good hand. "You can have this," she said, holding it out.

The Bigfoot grabbed the bag from her, and she fell forward. Her face landed against the creature's leg. She felt its muscles move as the creature took a step back. It raised one of its gigantic feet, and for a moment she believed that it was going to step on her. Zach called out her name and she heard the Bigfoot roar. She rolled away, almost into the water, and looked up to see that he had sprayed the bear spray at its face and upper abdomen.

The Bigfoot wiped at its eyes with the stump of its other arm. Zach, knowing he had not sprayed close enough to blind the creature, stepped over to Autumn and stood in front of her. The creature looked at them, wiping at its face again. It held the backpack up to its nose and sniffed. Its nostrils quivered, and it sniffed again. It let out a sad sound, almost like a sob.

"That's blood from its mate," Zach told the group. "We got it when we were in the cave."

"That's the body George saw," Carson realized. "A female Bigfoot."

Bigfoot looked at all of them, and they stopped talking. The creature roared again, as if challenging any of them to attack. They all stayed in one place. Autumn realized she was holding her breath, and let it out.

The creature kept its grip on the bag, and leapt back across the creek. They listened to its footsteps and the breaking foliage in its path until the gentle sound of the creek was the only sound left in the night. Autumn sat up, with Zach holding her close to him. All of her adrenaline suddenly dropped away.

"That's it, I'm done," Cal said. "I'm not messing with those things anymore."

"Wise idea," Reilly said as he and Carson finally crossed the creek and joined the others. Carson looked at Aaron, who was staring off in the direction that Bigfoot had gone.

"Are you okay?" he asked with concern in his voice. "Aaron?"

"I'm…I'm fine," Aaron replied slowly. He looked down at Tony's backpack. "You're taking this, aren't you?"

"Just what's inside," Carson said gently. "We'll need the bones to be tested sometime in the future."

"Okay," Aaron said. His voice sounded dazed. "The skin sample, too?"

"Both items belong to a private collection," Carson said. "Tony already tested what was sent to him. That's enough."

"Enough?" Cal said. "You can't keep that hidden away."

"We can, and we will," Reilly said. "I suggest you gentlemen check on Tony, go back to your cabin, and leave town as soon as possible."

"Is that an order?" Cal asked.

"It's a firm request," Reilly said. "We'll check on you to make sure you don't have any trouble finding your way down the highway."

"It's done," Aaron said. He turned to look at Cal. "Let's go." He crossed the creek, and the two men disappeared around the edge of the cabin. Zach heard them shout and saw them start running, but turned his attention to Autumn.

"Autumn, are you okay?" Zach asked. He could feel her body shaking against him.

"That was so close," she said with tears in her voice. "It could have really done some damage. It could have killed me so easily. It came here because it smelled something familiar and was looking for its mate, hoping she was still alive."

"Hopefully it will stay where it's supposed to be now," Reilly said. "Down at the cave."

"What about the dogman?" Autumn asked. "Last I saw, it was still alive."

Zach's heart sank, but he kept his hold on her. "There's nothing we can do about it, Autumn. If it's been wounded enough to die, it will die. If it survives, then we'll probably hear occasional reports of sightings."

"I think I've had enough close encounters with monsters for now," Autumn said. Her words brought some relief to Zach.

"Let's hope everyone else here feels the same," Carson said grimly. "I think we should get out of here."

They crossed the creek and made their way back to the front of the cabin. Autumn's friends saw them and rushed across the clearing. She sat on the porch and they stood in front of her and Zach. "What happened?" Erica asked. Bill kept his arm around her. Autumn saw that and smiled. Bill had been keeping his crush on Erica a secret for a long time.

Before Autumn could explain, Carson looked over at the other cabin and saw Tony sitting on the chair. He went over and examined him. He said a few things to Cal and Aaron while Mitzi and Marvin strolled over to Cabin One. "Everything okay here?" Marvin called out. Autumn noticed that they had come down here in a golf cart with the resort logo.

"Everything's fine now," Reilly assured them.

"We got some calls from the other guests about the howls and roars they were hearing," Marvin explained. "I told them they should stay inside for the night."

"We heard gun shots," Mitzi added. "And then Erica called us to ask for some help." She smiled. "Did you kill something?"

"I shot at an animal," Reilly said. "It was acting weird and being a nuisance. You can tell your guests that we took care of the problem."

"Good," she said.

"We'll get out of your way," Marvin added. "See you all tomorrow."

Everyone nodded. Carson spoke with the couple, removed a couple of items from Tony's bag, and then Mitzi and Marvin left with Tony and his friends in the cart for the short trip back to their cabin. Autumn suddenly let out a hysterical laugh. Zach leaned against her and she sighed, trying to calm down. She turned back to Erica.

"Bigfoot went after Aaron because it smelled the blood on my old backpack," she said. "The creature has the pack, Tony and his friends have been told to leave, and everything should hopefully quiet down here now."

"We saved Tony from the dogman again," Nate noted. "Given the two times it's been tased so far, I think it'll try to stay away from people if it can."

"Good," Zach said. "Let nature take care of it."

"How was Tony?" Autumn asked.

"Possible concussion and fracture in his arm," Carson said. "I told them to pack up tonight, stop at the clinic, and then leave."

"I think it's time to head back into town," Reilly said. "We'll be in touch tomorrow, Zach. And we will make sure Tony leaves after Carson examines him."

Zach nodded. "Thanks for your help tonight. All of it." He knew what they had risked by showing him the vault, and he appreciated it. He'd find a way to work some of it into the show without revealing exactly where he had viewed it.

"I'm very relieved we retrieved the bone and the skin sample," Carson said. "I think we'll be using a different lab for tests in the future."

At that point, Nate grabbed his shirt from the porch railing. "I was wearing this when we went after the dogman. You may find it useful."

"Thank you," Reilly said. He retrieved a plastic bag and placed the shirt inside, then placed the bone and the skin sample in bags as well and set them down in the car.

"Hey, did you mean what you told Cal? You consider everything in the vault to be a private collection?" Zach said quietly to Carson.

Carson drew Zach aside. "Yes. Reilly and I had it passed down to us from a previous clinic doctor and sheriff's deputy. I don't know yet if we'll pass it down in a similar fashion, but I think we should consider someday leaving it in the hands of someone who will appreciate it for what it is and not try to commercialize it."

He looked meaningfully at Zach. "You'd give it to me?" he asked quietly. He was overwhelmed.

"Just a consideration," Carson said. "I'd have to consult a few other people. Think about whether or not you'd want such a collection, though, and someday you'll have an answer when I approach you again."

Zach nodded. Carson clasped his shoulder, then redirected him back to the group. He and Reilly drove away, and Zach smiled tiredly at the others. "How about we meet tomorrow to discuss what's next?" he asked. "I think we've all had enough excitement."

"Agreed," Mike said. Nate, Bill, Mike, and Erica said goodnight and returned to their cabin. Zach helped Autumn up and inside the cabin, where she collapsed into tears on the couch.

"I don't know why I'm crying," she said. "So many Bigfoot hunters would have loved to be in my shoes tonight."

"They should be careful what they wish for," Zach told her. "One move, and you'd be gone. Injured, or dead. That's why I only wanted to observe before we came out here."

"We went after it this afternoon," she pointed out.

"Yes. And we got some good evidence," Zach admitted. "But I think we have enough footage for the show. So, let's head home tomorrow."

She nodded. "Okay. Thanks for bringing me to my senses

tonight."

"Always," Zach said, and kissed her. She went upstairs, and he stayed on the couch for a few moments.

He was exhausted, yet still felt he was being watched. He went around and closed the curtains. Before shutting the blinds on the side window, he saw a tall shape trying to hide next to a tree in the woods. A long snout was visible, sniffing the air. Zach closed the blinds and shut the curtains. He would not engage with any more monsters tonight.

CHAPTER 17

The next morning, Zach woke up to voices outside. He looked around the curtain and saw that Reilly and Joey were on the other side of the creek. Carson was there, too. Zach was surprised to also see George and Stan sitting down on stumps, watching the activity. He left Autumn sleeping, quickly got dressed, and dashed down the stairs. At the last second, he grabbed his camera. Something had happened over in that clearing, and he wanted to see what was going on.

George's truck was parked in front of the cabin, and so were a sheriff's cruiser and a van that Zach recognized as belonging to the medical clinic. He saw Mike and Nate looking out of the window from the other cabin. They raised their arms as if asking him a question. He shrugged and walked around the corner of the cabin.

The small crowd turned to watch Zach as he stepped across the water, careful about using the wet rocks to cross the creek. They were all standing by the branch shelter, and Joey immediately moved to block whatever had caught their interest from Zach's sight. Stan was still relaxing on a stump, but George was now standing next to him. "What's going on?" Zach asked them.

"I hear you had some excitement over here last night," Stan said. "Any chance you checked the footage near my house?"

"No," Zach said. "We were too busy. Why?"

"I saw Bigfoot walking down the gravel road in front of my house, right out in the open. It was carrying a bag of some sort, and walking slowly. When it reached my driveway, it stopped and sniffed the hedges, then kept going. I haven't seen it since."

"Let's keep it that way," George said. "I hope you don't mind, Zach, but I took it upon myself to save you a trip and took down your cameras. Four of them, right?"

"Yes. You got the video camera by the cave, too?"

"Yep." George then pulled something out of his coat pocket. Zach recognized it was one of his cameras. "This was the one that was out by the highway. We think the Bigfoot saw it and tore it down." He handed it to Zach in three pieces.

"Thanks." Autumn had briefly said something about one of the cameras before falling asleep last night, but he hadn't paid much attention. It was just equipment, and he could eventually replace it.

Zach had been thinking about leaving at least one of the cameras up for a few months, to continue his observation, but he kept that to himself. It was Stan's land, and he wanted to continue to be welcomed in the area. If he was covertly watching the cave, he somehow knew that when the camera was eventually found, the response to it would not be good for him.

"Thanks" he said. He walked over to the shelter, or as close as Reilly and Carson would allow him to get to it. "What's going on over here?"

"It's already gone," Carson said. "Joey, you might as well let him see."

"See what?" Zach asked. The deputies moved aside and let him look around the edge of the shelter.

A bloody mess had been left behind. Zach knew the shelter had been too small for the Bigfoot, although it appeared to have been created by one. His arm automatically brought the camera up to take pictures, but something stopped him. He shook his head. "Did something die here?" he asked.

Large patches of hair had been caught on the edge of the shelter, and Reilly was now collecting them and placing them in a bag. "We found the dogman here this morning," he said quietly. "I was curious about whether or not I had mortally wounded it last night. Joey volunteered to check the area with me and we saw the creature sleeping in here. When we approached, it stood up and lurched away. I chose not to follow it, but called Carson in case he thought we could do anything for it."

"I'm going to say no," Carson said. "It's an injured animal that may still have some fight in it. It's also still healing from another injury, and seemed to be strong even while dealing with that trauma. When I got here the creature was hanging out near the edge of the clearing. I turned to get a closer look at the shelter, and by the time we all turned around the dogman had disappeared."

"I suggest that we leave it be," Stan said, still sitting on the stump. "Let nature take care of it, even if nature may not have created it."

"I agree," Zach said, and they all looked surprised. "If it survives, I'm guessing it's going to be looking for a quieter, less populated area to live."

He helped Reilly, Carson, and Joey finish collecting the hair samples, then found the bloodiest branches and tossed them deeper into the forest. Zach looked around the clearing and decided that while he and Autumn were here, he may as well get an introduction to Tahoma Valley on film. This would be a peaceful spot, with the back of the shelter behind him as a great reminder of the creatures in the area.

They all crossed back over the creek. The deputies left to continue their patrol for the day. Carson drove the van away from the cabins without another word. Zach figured the doctor was anxious to get back to his normal routine.

Autumn had woken up, and she was sitting on the porch, still in sweatpants and t-shirt, with Talia when Zach returned to the cabin. George and Stan returned to their truck, but didn't leave. They seemed to be waiting to talk Zach again.

"I just came by to apologize again," Talia said. "I wish you luck with your adventures in looking for cryptids."

"Thank you," Zach said. "You really did have an interesting story on your own."

"I know something big happened here last night," Talia said. "Tony and his friends looked exhausted when they came back last night. I could hear the howls and roars, and even a couple of shots. Cal got busy packing up their car, and they left with a sheriff's deputy following them."

"Tony got injured last night during an encounter with Bigfoot, and Marvin and Mitzi came out to help get him back to his cabin," Zach said. "They said quite a few people at the resort heard the same things you did. You were wise to stay inside."

"I've started doing some reading about Bigfoot," Talia confessed. "I can see why people become interested in it." She stood. She was fully dressed and carried her purse with her. "It's been an interesting couple of days. Thanks for setting me straight about Tony. I've always tried to avoid people like him."

"He wants the same answers we do," Zach said. "He just chose the wrong way to go about it this time."

"I'm guessing that whatever happened over here had something to do with that backpack he was carrying around," Talia said.

"You noticed that?" Autumn asked.

Talia explained Tony's strange behavior the day before. "I'm just glad to be done with him." She flashed a smile at Zach. "Autumn told me you're filming a new season of your show soon. By the time it's on, I'll probably be caught up on the previous seasons."

"I'm always glad to meet a new fan," Zach laughed.

"Don't be afraid to reach out if you ever need any questions answered regarding what's known about Bigfoot or other monsters," Autumn told her.

"I will," Talia promised. "I'm heading out now. Time to get back to my life." She got into her car and drove away.

George and Stan were still waiting by Stan's truck. Zach and Autumn walked over to them. "Here are your cameras," George said, picking up one of them.

Autumn smiled. "Is there any way we could keep one of the still cameras up on your property? Just to see if we can get any glimpses of one of the creatures if they appear?"

George looked at his father. "It's your property, Dad. You decide."

Stan looked at the cameras. "Where do you want to put it?"

"At the start of the trail leading to the cave," Zach said. He hugged Autumn from the side. "I was thinking of asking that, but she beat me to it."

"Sure," Stan agreed.

Zach glanced at the cameras and only saw two of them. "We're missing one," he said.

George looked at the truck bed. "I may have accidentally left one up already."

Stan laughed. "I figured you would. Keep an eye on that trail, Zach. Please keep me updated if you see anything strange."

"I will." Stan and George got into their truck and waved goodbye.

The rest of the morning was spent packing. Mike and Bill headed out to the clearing and returned with the gear they had left behind the previous night. They also came back with dirt samples that included dogman blood, which Autumn tucked away for future use, along with photos of a bloody trail leading into the forest. Erica and Autumn checked the camera footage Stan had mentioned and saw the Bigfoot returning to the cave. It held the bag up into the air and whooped three times, as if celebrating something, then walked back into the cave. The next several minutes of video were dark, and then the entire screen went blank.

Zach sat at the kitchen table in his cabin for a couple of hours. He examined the footage from the trail camera at the back of the cabin. It had picked up everyone crossing the creek, a couple of grainy shots of Bigfoot as an almost hidden shape in the trees, and then everyone returning from the clearing. He went out and took down the camera, then returned to the table to focus on the next part of the project.

He wrote down some thoughts of what he wanted to say about what was hiding in Tahoma Valley on camera. He was only interrupted once, when Autumn's friends came over to let them know they were leaving. Autumn promised Erica she'd let her know when they got home, and they left chatting excitedly about what they'd have to write about on the BOG forum later that day.

Zach finished writing. He and Autumn packed up their leftover food, then washed the dishes and made sure everything was packed away and clean before locking the door to the cabin. Autumn carried the video camera across the creek and they set it up facing the branch shelter. The area was quiet, except for the normal forest sounds. They were reassuring to Zach.

"Before we start recording, I want to talk to you about something," Zach said. Autumn sat down next to him on a stump.

"What is it?"

"Last night, Carson hinted that someday I may get the collection I saw in the vault yesterday."

"You didn't tell me what you saw there," she pointed out. "We were kind of interrupted by monsters."

He described the vault and the history of the pictures, footprint casts, and the other items that had been included. He included the locked doors, the controlled temperature, and the bigger items like the preserved hand and the bones that had been found this summer. "It was incredible. They really take care of the collection. I know some things may have come into the collection by covert means, like some of the pictures that were taken from phones and cameras that people later reported missing after Bigfoot encounters. I can see why Carson and Reilly think it's worth keeping secret and protecting for as long as they can. Really, it's a perfect timeline for a history of Bigfoot in the area."

"We've been looking for a topic for the book we want to write," she pointed out. "Do you think they'd let you back down there to make more notes and do some research?"

"Limited access, maybe," he said. "At least while the collection still exists here in town. We'd still have to seek out information in other places. It's worth asking about. I really need to start thinking about what I'm eventually going to do with my life. The show isn't going to last forever."

"No, but given what you've learned during your time on the show, I imagine you'll probably be in demand for similar projects."

Zach hugged and kissed her. "In the meantime, we still have this episode to work on. Let's do it." He stood up and positioned himself with his back to the small tree shelter. It was a cloudy day, and cool, so he put on his *Creature Hunt* sweatshirt. He faced Autumn and the camera. It was a perfect moment, quiet and still with the gentle rushing of the creek providing a serene background.

"Ready?" Autumn asked. He nodded, and she pressed the button to record him.

"Welcome to the town of Tahoma Valley. It's a small place, close to Mount Rainier, and is a popular spot for tourists. People love to stay and shop here, using it as a base for exploring the mountain. But there's a darker presence in Tahoma Valley, one that occasionally makes itself felt in big ways.

"For some time now, I have been reading reports, detailed reports, of Bigfoot sightings coming from this area. A couple of years ago, I was lucky enough to witness the creature in person, and have close contact with it. Recently, I have come across the creature again, and another cryptid along with it. There have been rumors that an upright walking canine, popularly known as a dogman, has been living in these woods, as well."

Zach pointed to the structure behind him. "What created this shelter? What creatures have been seen lately prowling around dumpsters, rummaging through campsites, and leaving large footprints behind as they once again disappear into the darkness? Join me as we explore the forests around Tahoma Valley to see if Bigfoot really exists here. We'll examine evidence taken from years of sightings and determine if a dogman has recently made this peaceful town his home as well. Come along with me as, together, we go on our next creature hunt."

A long, mournful howl pierced the air. It was followed seconds later by a couple of long whoops. It was a perfect end to the introduction.

Autumn turned off the camera. "That will get everyone's attention. This is going to be a great episode."

Zach smiled.

ABOUT THE AUTHOR

C.E. Osborn grew up in Tacoma, Washington, and currently resides in New Jersey. She is a cataloging librarian and enjoys reading mysteries and stories about cryptid creatures. You can learn more at www.ceosborn.wordpress.com and on Facebook.

Works by C.E. Osborn

Tahoma Valley
Days of Halloween
Trail of Monsters
Wolf Crossing
October Nights
Creature Hunt
Circle of Darkness
Shadow in the Trees
Camp Thunder Cloud

Poetry:
Dream Softly
Before You Take My Hand

Lonely Hollow series:
Secret Hollow
Stormy Hollow
Winter Hollow
Lonely Hollow

Printed in Great Britain
by Amazon